A Hidden Death At San Francisco
A Father Ibarra California Missions Mystery

Sunstone books may be purchased for educational, business, or sales promotional use.
For information please write: Special Markets Department, Sunstone Press,
P.O. Box 2321, Santa Fe, New Mexico 87504-2321.

Book and cover design › R. Ahl
Printed on acid-free paper
∞
eBook 978-1-61139-207-4

Library of Congress Cataloging-in-Publication Data

Names: O'Hagan, John J., author.
Title: A hidden death at San Francisco : a Father Ibarra California
  missions mystery / by John J. O'Hagan.
Description: Santa Fe, NM : Sunstone Press, [2021] | Includes readers'
  guide. | Summary: "The Death of a Native American from Mission San
  Francisco leads to a trip of discovery through California's Delta for a
  Franciscan priest in the 18th century"-- Provided by publisher.
Identifiers: LCCN 2021013544 | ISBN 9781632933201 (paperback) | ISBN
  9781611392074 (epub)
Subjects: LCGFT: Detective and mystery fiction.
Classification: LCC PS3615.H33 H53 2021 | DDC 813/.6--dc23
LC record available at https://lccn.loc.gov/2021013544

WWW.SUNSTONEPRESS.COM
SUNSTONE PRESS / POST OFFICE BOX 2321 / SANTA FE, NM 87504-2321 /USA
(505) 988-4418 / FAX (505) 988-1025

A HIDDEN DEATH AT SAN FRANCISCO
A Father Ibarra California Missions Mystery

John J. O'Hagan

SUNSTONE PRESS

SANTA FE

Dedication

To the fair Letitia, who read, and re-read, and read again.
With all my love.

¤ PREFACE

This book is a work of fiction, but as with most fiction, it is based on certain well-documented facts.

Under the realm of fact in this book: The Franciscans, in their seventy-five years establishing and running the California missions, were scrupulous record-keepers. We know the names—and to a very large measure the activities, both good and bad—of the 142 Franciscan priests who served in the missions.

Of all the California missions, Mission San Francisco was the one most frequently troubled by disease and epidemics. Because of these diseases, it was also the mission most plagued with problems of escapism, as its native population fled the unhealthy environs. Two Franciscan priests assigned to San Francisco, Fathers Antonio Danti and Martin de Landaeta, were unrelenting in their pursuit of any of the "neophytes" who tried to leave the mission.

In 1795, during one of these expeditions, several of the Indians in Father Danti's party were killed. As a result of this, the governor of California issued an order against any further such efforts.

Despite this prohibition, a year later Danti embarked on another such expedition. When he heard of this, the governor ordered a full investigation into the goings-on at San Francisco. That investigation led to the discovery of a systemic pattern of abuse and cruelty. Fathers Danti and de Landaeta were both removed from their positions and returned to the Franciscan college in Mexico City.

Under the realm of fiction: There was never a Franciscan priest named Juan José Ibarra assigned to the California missions, nor was there ever a Franciscan priest who was also a physician assigned to these missions.

The two men, priest and soldier, walked carefully through the fading darkness of the early morning. They had a general idea of where they were heading, but the darkness and the fog made each step a tentative one. They knew what they were looking for—the grave—which they had carefully marked the evening before. Given the trouble they had experienced in finding it, they had marked it with a stack of logs and branches. They were not quite sure, though, exactly where that marker was in this damp, unearthly light. Everything around them faded into a gray sameness. Both were keenly aware of the fact that what they were actually searching for was a man who had been dead for almost a year. The enveloping fog, sodden sounds of their progress, and the eerie, pre-dawn silence were not in any way reassuring in the grim task.

Suddenly the soldier stopped and, nudging the priest, pointed ahead. There, rising through the swirling fog, was an irregular, indistinct shape.

I didn't realize we had piled the markers quite that high, the friar thought, *but that has to be the grave.* They moved toward it, and were almost upon it when the shape moved, shifted and stood larger. The young soldier gave a sharp intake of breath as a shrouded figure turned to them.

"Estella," the priest gasped. "You have been here all night?"

The young lady pulled the shawl back from her head. "Yes, Father, I have been here all night. I have found my husband after a year, and I will not leave him again until he is in holy ground."

It was a late May afternoon when one of the mission Indians brought him a letter from Monterey. Letters from the capitol were not a rare event at Mission San Miguel, but letters addressed to Fr. Juan José Ibarra were. With equal parts curiosity and foreboding, he took the unopened document out to the crisp sunshine of the courtyard. Looking to the line of trees to the east, which he knew marked the Salinas River, he held the parchment in his hand while he contemplated not just the scene, but his life.

Trained as a physician in Spain before coming to Alta California, his primary role was to bring relief to the natives who suffered greatly from the Spanish conquest. A rigidly enforced new lifestyle, and the introduction of new diseases, had not been a happy combination for the native Californians. Father Ibarra's task was to alleviate and if possible, to eliminate the suffering caused by these circumstances.

That had not been easy to achieve. As that rare creature, a physician on the edge of the Spanish empire, he had found that both the military and civilian bureaucracy always seemed to find reasons to keep him busy with their own complaints. Now, after five years of great effort, he was finally establishing a base of patients for the Indians at Mission San Miguel. San Miguel was an ideal location that seemed to meet everyone's needs. It was close enough to the capitol at Monterey, so that the demands of the military and civilian rulers could be met. At the same time, it was far enough away so that those demands would not be a daily burden. There was a large population of natives at several missions clustered around the capitol, and there were also fairly large settlements of unconverted natives who could benefit from his skills.

But best of all, in one of the Salinan villages he had found a native shaman who was willing to share her knowledge of local cures and, just as importantly, was willing to consider his knowledge of European medicine. He and the shaman, Kaya, had formed a unique partnership. As a healer of the Salinan people, she had a long-established relationship of trust with her people. Father Juan had found many of her treatments amazingly effective, and while never spurning his Old World medical training, he had not hesitated to use her New World cures, amazingly effective in bringing relief to the suffering. While she treated primarily the natives in the surrounding areas and he tended to missionaries and soldiers, all benefited from the melding of the two worlds. Several of the Spanish soldiers and bureaucracy, unbeknownst to them, had been cured of a nagging illness by a potion from "Father Juan's witchdoctor," while several of the natives had gotten from their shaman the benefits of the latest European medical knowledge.

He glanced down at the still unopened letter. Was this going to be the end of those efforts? Where was he being sent now? He had landed originally at San Diego. San Diego had led to Monterey, and Monterey to San Miguel. Where now? Resigned to the fact that only by opening the letter would he know, Father Juan broke the seal. He first looked down to the bottom of the second page at the elaborate signature. That brought him no comfort. There was not one signature, but two: Diego de Borica, governor of Alta California; and Fermin Francisco de Lasuen, father president of the Franciscan missionaries of California. A letter from the two most powerful men in Alta California could not possibly be good news.

As he began reading the letter, he recognized the familiar scrawl of Father Lasuen, his superior:

My dear brother in Christ.

Greetings to you and blessings to the wonderful work you are accomplishing among our neophytes and their unconverted gentile brothers. I, and as you will note by the additional signature on this letter, the esteemed governor general of Alta California, have need of your services at our Mission San Francisco de Assisi located in the town of Yerba Buena, to the north of you.

More than any of us, you know one of the most troubling aspect of our efforts to convert the natives of Alta California has been their weakness of health. Sickness and disease visit these unfortunates in a devastating fashion. Of course, that is the primary reason you have been sent to help us. As a physician, you have the skills necessary to help us find answers to these problems.

Here the priest could not help but ruefully shake his head. For several years he had been trying to point out to his superiors that the illnesses that did indeed decimate the converted population in Alta California had very little effect on the larger number of natives who persisted in living outside the mission system. Although he was not totally sure of exact cause and effect, he had more than once suggested that the crowded and unhygienic living conditions of the mission Indians was responsible. His suggestions had gone unheeded.

Of all of our missions, San Francisco de Assisi is most affected. The neophytes adamantly refuse to stay there. They flee in such large numbers that the mission industries, particularly weaving and shoemaking, have trouble meeting the quotas required by the army.

There it is, Father Ibarra thought. *The concern is not that the Indians are dying, but that the mission may be losing some income.* He read on.

I ask you, Fray, for the good of our order and for the good of those unfortunate Indians who are suffering, as soon as possible to put your work at San Miguel on hold, and proceed north to San Francisco de Assisi. Arriving there, offer your services to Father Martin de Landaeta, the superior at that mission. This letter will serve as your commission from both myself and the governor of Alta California in this task. You are not being assigned to Mission San Francisco de Assisi as a member of that staff; rather, you are being ordered by myself and the governor to expend your time and your efforts in arriving at the cause of their persistent sickness, and to offer your expertise towards a solution.

Here, the script changed to an unfamiliar one.

I, Diego de Borica, Governor of Alta California, do commission Father Juan José Ibarra as my personal representative in this matter; and I order all persons, civilian and military, to give him maximum assistance in this regard.

Father Ibarra studied again the two elaborate signatures. Even without the second signature, his own vow of obedience dictated that a request from a superior was an order. Given the additional endorsement of Governor Borica, he was now under obedience not just to the cross, but to the crown. He would have to make arrangements and travel to San Francisco "as soon as possible."

It was less than two weeks later when the Spanish ship *Princessa* beat past the headlands of Point Bonita and Point Lobos. Standing on the deck and watching the water trail past the sides was Father Ibarra. He was still slightly overwhelmed at the pace of events that had brought him here. As he traveled north from San Miguel to Monterey, he had stopped at the capitol to receive final instructions. At his meeting with the governor, an aide had pointed out that the next day a ship was scheduled to sail from Monterey to San Francisco. Rather than continuing north by mule for another ten days, the father could be there in less than a week travelling on her majesty's ship *Princessa*. Governor Borica had immediately seized on the idea and made everything happen with head-spinning speed.

Father Ibarra had been told by the bustling sailors that they were sailing into the greatest port known, "a harbor that could hold all of the ships in the world." Whether that was true or not he had no way of knowing, since he could not see anything in the swirling fog beyond the ship's bowsprit. In fact, for the past several days all he had seen was fog. The ship which had left Monterey under a brilliant sun and blue skies had seen neither sun nor sky almost as soon as they cleared the shallow arc of Monterey Bay. Now, arrived at their destination, it seemed as if what awaited them was more fog and dampness. Father Juan, who in his brief time in California had begun to equate the region with sunshine and warmth, tried to reassure himself. It was, after all, winter, and even California must have a winter.

Shortly after sailing through the narrow opening to the bay, the ship turned sharply to the right. Sails were lowered and reefed. A longboat with tow lines was put down, and the ship was laboriously and slowly pulled ahead. Finally, the priest saw hills looming out of the fog, and the shadowy outline of a military fort. An anchor was dropped. With the ship secured, the captain came down from the quarter deck and addressed the priest.

"Well, Father," he said, "if you will go to your cabin and get your things, we'll take you ashore to the *presidio*. We'll get your other luggage and supplies to you as soon as possible. You should plan to spend the night there, and tomorrow you'll be given an escort to Mission San Francisco. It is a very short distance from the *presidio*."

This was probably the longest conversation the captain had engaged in with the priest since they had left Monterey. He had made no secret of his firm belief that a priest on a ship was worse luck than a woman. The governor had ordered him to deliver Father Ibarra to San Francisco, and that having been accomplished, he did not intend to keep him aboard any longer than was absolutely necessary. Already, the boat that had guided the ship to its anchorage was pulling alongside in anticipation of its next task: delivering the priest to shore. Father Juan hurried to his cabin, secured the trunk he had packed on arising that morning, and returned with it to the deck. One of the sailors took the trunk and disappeared over the side with it. Making his way to the railing, Father Juan looked down and saw the man with a one-handed grip at the bottom of a rope ladder, his trunk on his shoulder. He handed the trunk to one of his companions in the boat and scrambled back up to the deck.

"*Vaya con Dios,* Father. Please, your blessing before you leave." The sailor swept the hat from his head and knelt reverently. While the captain had been uncommunicative and surly, the sailors had been open and friendly to the priest during the voyage. They were uneducated men, and they were deferential and respectful to a distinguished passenger who was not just a priest, but a physician. To them, such qualifications were almost godlike. Most of them would never in their life meet a physician, and the priests they met seemed only to be interested in reminding them of the torments of hell that awaited them. Father Juan had never chastised them. He enjoyed visiting with them in their brief periods of rest. He listened to their tales, laughed at their jokes and sympathized with their harsh life. Injuries were an everyday occurrence of their life and most often they were left to heal on their own. With Father Juan aboard, the sailors got used to bringing cuts, sores and even broken bones to him. He tended them and patched them and gave them a few moments of respite from their harsh and brutal life. Now he was leaving them.

Father Juan extended his hand over the sailor's bowed head and, making the sign of the cross over him, intoned, "*In nomine Patris, et Filius, et Spritus Sanctus…*" He turned, tucked his grey robes around him, and climbed awkwardly over the side and down the ladder.

¤ 4

Two days later, Father Juan was settled at Mission San Francisco de Assisi. He had been welcomed to the mission by Father Martin de Landaeta. Father de Landaeta, enthusiastic at meeting what he considered a new member for his struggling team, was somewhat less than enthusiastic on being informed that Father Juan was not there as an addition to the mission staff, but rather as a physician who had been sent by both the governor of California and the president of the Franciscans to seek some answer to the twin problems of disease and escapism that so plagued San Francisco.

"They are a weak and indolent people," Father de Landaeta said. He had welcomed Fr. Juan into the small cell that served as an office. "They reject our way of life and refuse to work to harvest their own food. It is for this reason that they become sick. It is well known that sickness and runaways plague all of the missions, not just San Francisco."

"You are right, Father." Father Juan answered. He realized that he was inserting himself into the absolute domain of the other priest. There was probably no more independent nor absolute fiefdom existing than that of one of the California missions. Although each mission's superior was subject to the word of the father president, that word was several weeks away from ever being delivered, and time and distance made each mission's superior pretty much his own master.

Fr. Juan continued carefully. "Sickness and desertion of those we have been sent to save *is* a problem at all of the missions. It was for this very reason that I have been sent to Alta California. The order has decided that the services of a physician might be of help in addressing this problem. We have to start somewhere, and in fact, while it is true that this problem is not unique to San Francisco, at San Francisco the problem is by far worse than it is at any other mission."

Father de Landaeta seemed a bit taken aback at this information, but he remained silent.

"Thus, I have been ordered by both the governor and the father president to base myself in San Francisco, at least for the time, and to begin seeking an answer to this problem."

As he knew it would, the mention to Father de Landaeta of the two most important powers in Alta California effectively ended any discussion of his duties.

"Of course, Father, of course, we will make every effort to help you in your search for an answer to this unfortunate situation. What is it we can do to help you with this?"

"Well," Father Juan continued, "I will need a small office or space to work in, aside from my cell. Also, if you have a bright and helpful young man who could assist me, one who speaks Spanish as well as his own tongue, that would be helpful. I can speak the language of several of the tribes to the south, but those from this area are foreign to me."

The superior interrupted him. "All of our neophytes can speak Spanish. They may not like to admit that, but it is true. They are instructed in our faith in Spanish and they must demonstrate a knowledge of the elements of that faith before they are baptized and brought into full communion."

"I understand that," Father Juan explained. "But my study of the question of diseases among the natives will involve my examination of not just neophytes, but gentiles as well. It is fairly obvious that there are distinct differences in the disease experience between those who have been converted and those who have chosen to continue as children of nature. I will need help in querying some of the people in the outlying villages who very well may not speak Spanish, or," he continued "will not be eager to admit that they do." He hurried on without allowing the other priest to comment further. "Aside from a little space and an interpreter, once my books and supplies are brought from the ship, I will have all I need."

The superior smiled and nodded slightly. "That can all be arranged. I will have one of our storage rooms cleared or re-arranged so that you can use it as an office. As far as an assistant, I think perhaps Guillermo would be a good choice. He is a bright young man and has no family; they have all died in one of the unfortunate diseases we have been discussing. There are some of us who think that we should perhaps consider him for Holy Orders. I cannot say that I necessarily agree with that high opinion, but his work with you can only enhance his education." He gestured out the office door and to the south. "The room, if you would like to examine it, is down the colonnade on the left side of the church. It looks out on the courtyard and the cemetery ground. We should have it ready for you tomorrow, and I will send a messenger to the *presidio* this afternoon, to see about your other things from the ship." He paused, and Juan wondered what emotion was hidden in that pause. "Welcome to Mission Dolores, Father."

Father Juan was preparing to leave, but turned again to the older priest. "You know, Father, I am intrigued by that nickname. This is the only one of the missions I have heard so often referred to by a name other than its own. *Dolores*: what an unhappy appellation. Is this in fact a place of such pain that it deserves that name?"

Father de Landaeta smiled tightly and replied, "Oh no, Father, I don't think this is such a place. You know this is one of the very few missions sited by the military and not by our order. They chose the location on the feast day of Our Lady of Sorrows, and so named a small creek and lake which you will soon discover. The name has become attached to our Mission San Francisco de Assisi."

"Interesting," Father Juan commented. "A saint who tried to bring joy and peace to the world has his mission nicknamed 'pains.' Good night, Father. I look forward to my time here."

¤ 5

It was only a few days later that Father Juan had his concerns about the sorrows of Mission Dolores raised again. A young Ohlone woman came to see him. She couldn't have been twenty years old. She had, in a cotton sling around her shoulders, an infant of probably less than a year. In the priest's view, she was a child holding a child. She was dressed in the plain linen shift worn by all the neophyte women. Her glossy black hair was cut in a short bob with bangs. She approached the priest hesitantly, deep black eyes wide with apprehension.

"*Buenas dias, Padre,*" she greeted him. "My name is Estella. I am one of the neophytes here at Mission San Francisco. Guillermo has told us that we should talk to you if we think something is wrong."

"*Si, hija,* what can I do for you? Have a seat, please." He gestured toward one of the chairs in his small office. The young woman sat tentatively on the edge of the chair. She rearranged the sling and settled the sleeping child in her lap. She fixed the priest with an intense stare. Father Juan realized that she was waiting for him to speak first.

"What is it, my dear? Are you sick? Is the child sick?" he asked.

"No, no, Father, we are well. It is…" She left the sentence unfinished.

"Would you like me to get Guillermo to be here?" the priest asked. "Would you like me to get another woman here to be with us?"

The girl sighed. "No, Father, that is not necessary. It is about my husband. I would like to ask you to help me with my husband."

Father Juan groaned inwardly. Domestic problems were not something he was at all qualified to speak to. A sick woman, a sick child, perhaps a sick husband he could deal with, but he had the decided impression that this lady was not here to talk about illness. Desperately he asked, "Is your husband ill? Is there something I can do to help him?"

Suddenly tears welled up in the girl's eyes. "My husband is dead, Father."

Before he could question this startling revelation, she continued. "My husband was chosen last year to go on an expedition with Father Danti. He did not come back. Father Danti told me that he had gotten sick and died. He told me that he was buried by the priests and the soldiers so that his disease would not spread to the others. He was buried where he died, in the *pantanos*."

The answer, rather than easing Father Juan's discomfort, added to it. He quickly checked the urge to respond automatically, *If your husband is dead, Señora, I will pray for him. There is not much else that can be done.* There was something in the woman's comment, and in her demeanor, that suggested to him there was more to her story.

"I am sorry, *hija*," he began. "What is it I can do for you?"

She hesitated only briefly and continued. "I do not think my husband died of disease, Father. Francisco was a young and healthy man. He had already survived several bouts of the 'mission sickness.' Since we were married, we have not been required to live in the mission quarters. We had our own house in the settlements outside of the mission. We were not near the people who were sick. He was not sick at all when he left on the expedition with Father Danti. After only four days, Father Danti and the others came back without Francisco. They told me he had gotten sick and died."

A thoroughly troubled Father Ibarra asked, "What is it that you think happened, my dear?"

"I do not know what happened," she answered vehemently. "That is what I am asking you to find out. What I know is that when Francisco left me and our child, he was healthy and happy. He told me he would be back in a week or ten days. He told me they were going across the bay, and up the river which the Spanish call the *San Joaquin*. They were going to find some neophytes who had run away. Xavier was with him, and several other neophytes whose names I do not know. There were soldiers with them, and Father Danti. Father Danti came back, the soldiers came back, Xavier came back. All came back except Francisco. They told me Francisco had gotten sick and died, and they buried him." She paused and took a deep breath. "I want to be taken to the place where he was buried, Father. Francisco and I are Catholics of this Mission San Francisco. Our son," she glanced down at the sleeping infant, "was baptized by Father de Landaeta. He must be able to visit his father, and to offer a prayer for him." She gave a slight sigh and used the moment to wipe ineffectively at the tears now running down her cheeks. "I am a good Catholic, Father. The priests have taught us that the dead are not really gone, they are part of us, and they can hear our prayers; we are to honor the dead. My son and I cannot do that if Francisco is buried in some unknown place in the swamps."

Father Juan considered what he had heard and asked again. "What is it you want me to do, my dear?"

The young woman stared down at her sleeping child and then back at the priest. "Guillermo has told us that you are not part of Mission San Francisco. He says that you have the power of the governor and of the father president. He says it is your job to find out what is making us sick and what is killing us. Well, Father, I have been told that my husband became sick and it killed him." Despite her tears and initial hesitancy in talking with the priest, she now fixed him with a gaze that could only be characterized as challenging. "I want you to find out what was that sickness that killed my husband. I also want him buried in holy ground at Mission San Francisco. I do not want him left in the *pantanos*."

Although Father Juan was doubtful about the extent of his "power of the governor" and even more unsure about his "power from the father president," he considered what the woman had said. He had been thinking since his arrival how he best might make some inroads with the natives at San Francisco. So far, nothing had come to him. The mission Indians were deferential and respectful, and the unconverted Indians sullen and withdrawn. Estella was now presenting him with perhaps the perfect opportunity. An opportunity, he realized, which, while fraught with difficulty, might finally be the door he was seeking to open. He spoke very cautiously, thinking his way through what he was saying.

"As you know, my dear, I am new to San Francisco. As I understand it, the expedition on which your husband died was many months ago."

"It was more than a year ago!" she interrupted without hesitation. "It was March of last year. It is now June of 1796."

Father Juan was struck by her grasp of exact dates. This was obviously a lady who had the event firmly fixed in her mind, who thought of it daily.

"Yes, a year ago. How can I discover a year later what sickness killed your husband? Who can tell me a year later what happened on that expedition?"

The young woman gathered the child to her and began to rise.

"Wait," Father Juan began. He put a very tentative hand on her arm. "Do not leave. I want to be sure you understand what a difficult task you are asking me to perform. I am not saying I will not try to help you."

"You are a priest, Father; do you not have special powers? I have been told that you are also a physician, that you can examine even one who is dead, and know what he died of."

Father Juan decided that now was not the time to discuss the special powers of the priesthood, but he felt he needed to address his skills as a physician. "A year, my dear..." he began, and then realized that he did not want to engage in a detailed conversation with this lady on the process of decomposition. "There are certain causes of death which can in fact be determined after death, but even the most skilled physician would have difficulty in determining which of many diseases might have killed a person a year later."

Estella seemed to be almost anticipating his answer. "Those certain causes of death that you *could* determine, what would some of those be?"

Father Juan struggled to come up with some answers. "Well," he began, "if a person fell from a great height, for example, many bones would be broken. If a person was beat with a club, the head and skull would be damaged. If a person was killed by a bear or other great beast, there would be teeth marks on the bones."

"What if a person was shot by a gun?" she asked.

"A gunshot? Yes. I think I could determine that. Are you telling me your husband was shot?"

Now the woman did stand to leave. "I *do not know* how my husband died," she emphasized. "But I do not think he died of disease." She finished settling the child in the sling, and headed towards the door. Before opening it, she turned once more. Father Juan was struck by the transformation that had taken place in his visitor. A confused and trembling young girl had come into his office. An imperious and demanding woman was preparing to leave. Her high cheekbones and glossy bangs accentuated her piercing, challenging stare.

"I will help you, Estella," he said. "I only ask that you give me the time I will need to answer some very difficult questions."

"It has been more than a year," the young lady answered. "I do not need an answer this week or next month. I just want an answer, and I want my husband back. *Buenas dias, Padre.*"

Father Juan stood at the narrow entrance to the bay on an afternoon that was finally sunny and clear. It had been several days since his conversation with Estella. He had thought, again and again, of her concerns, but he had done nothing positive to address them. He had promised himself that he would not leave his musings today without deciding the specific course he would embark on.

He watched the powerful swells roll in from the ocean. He had spent enough time on ships to know of the destruction and damage those waves could cause. These powerful waves, however, glistening green in the sunlight, did little more than cast a thin line of white surf at the edges of the rocks on either side of the narrow opening to the bay. They then spent themselves in joining the placid gloss of the huge harbor. It was as if after their long tumultuous journey across the ocean, they gave a sigh of relief and settled down to the comfort of their new home.

His mind turned again to his conversation with Estella. She had made it clear that she did not accept what she had been told of her husband's death. More disturbingly, she had at least implied that her husband had died violently; by a gunshot wound. If there was any basis for her concerns, she was seeking not merely answers to her questions; she was seeking justice. *I came here to resolve physical ills. Now I am being asked to address social or even criminal ills.*

Other than his conversation with Estella, he had heard only indirectly of the expedition on which her husband had died. There were short snatches of conversation among the Indians, a word here, a phrase there. If he tried to inquire further, he got only the standard, "Nothing, Father, you misunderstand us. There is nothing we were talking about that took place last year." Once he had the temerity to directly ask Father Danti what the Indians were referring to. The answer he got from the other priest was even more abrupt.

"They are discussing nothing!" the priest had insisted. "They are an idle people. They love to talk among themselves and invent stories." Noticing Juan's surprise at his forceful reply, he continued more calmly. "We have long had a problem with fugitives here at the mission. In the spring of last year, I and some soldiers tried to bring some of them back. We were unsuccessful, primarily because several of the Indians got sick and could not continue. The Indians have invented all sorts of fanciful stories as to why we failed. They will tell you of a great battle which ensued and in which the Indians defeated the soldiers, as if a bunch of savages armed with arrows and rocks could turn back the Spanish army. If you are going to believe everything you hear from the Indians in Alta California, Father, you will find your stay here very difficult indeed. Pay them no heed." Given the forcefulness of the Father Danti's response, Father Ibarra had pursued the question no further with him.

He could not put his conversation with the young Indian woman out of his mind, however. She had made no wild claim of battles or victory or defeat. She had simply said that there was an expedition, that at least one person had died during it, and that she did not find satisfying the explanation of that death. He dreaded the thought of bringing the subject up again with the priests at the mission, but he realized that if he was going to have any hope of answering her questions, he would have to do so, and not only with the priests, but with the Indians and the military as well. He could see an inevitable and uncomfortable confrontation looming. It was as inevitable as the progress of the waves he was watching. He gave a last glance at the bay, turned and started back to the mission. As he entered the compound he came across Guillermo.

"Guillermo," he asked, "come and visit with me. Come to my office." Entering the small room, the priest took the chair behind the writing table. He invited the young man to sit in the other chair. He took a journal from the desk and opened it, prepared to write. He addressed Guillermo.

"Some time ago, Guillermo, a young woman came to see me. Her name is Estella. She has presented me with an interesting challenge. In my efforts to meet that challenge I need to begin to understand what happened last year on an expedition to recover some fugitives."

Guillermo smiled broadly and sat back in his chair. "I know Estella," he said. "She does not believe the story of how her husband died. It was I who suggested she visit with you. I remember when they left on the expedition. It was early in March. We had just begun the Lent season. Many of the neophytes were sick and several had died. The people were afraid. Each night two or three neophytes would sneak away. So many left that it was hard to keep the looms and shops working. The fathers were very angry. They told the people who were left that they had to work longer. 'Blame your brothers who have left,' they said. 'It is because they have run away that you must do their work. If you don't want to work so hard, make them come back.' They also stopped the people from going to the bay or the hills to gather food. 'There is no time for that now,' they said, or, 'If we let you go to the hills you will just run away.' Nothing helped. The people kept running away. I tried to tell the fathers that their anger was only making things worse, that they were punishing those who stayed, and those punishments would just make more people leave."

Father Juan interrupted. "Oh? And what was their answer to that?"

Guillermo paused very briefly and continued. "They told me not to forget myself. That I was just an *Indio* and that it was not my job to tell the fathers how to run the mission." He shrugged. "After that I said no more. Finally, Father Danti convinced Father de Landaeta that by not going after the fugitives they were encouraging others to leave. 'They see that those who leave are just allowed to go, so they decide to leave as well. We must bring back some of the fugitives and punish them, and that way the others will be afraid to leave.' They talked with the soldiers at the *presidio*. At first the soldiers didn't want to go with them. They said, 'We are not supposed to be chasing Indians in the wilds. It is our job to guard the harbor and the mission.' Father Danti told them, 'That is all we are asking you to do. The priests are going to take a trip and we are asking you to go along to protect them. We are not asking you to chase or capture Indians. All the soldiers have to do is accompany us and protect us if we are attacked.' Finally, it was decided. Father Danti would lead an expedition to the *Rio San Joaquin*. Corporal Montoya would accompany him, with a squad of soldiers. I am not sure how many soldiers there were, maybe six or eight. Father de Landaeta would stay behind to supervise the mission. Father Danti took a bunch of neophytes, both from the mission and from the villages, maybe ten or twelve, I do not know all that he took."

Here, Father Juan interrupted him. "You were not on the expedition?"

"No, Father, I was not chosen to go on the expedition."

"Do you know the names of any who were? Can you tell me those names?"

"Well, I know he took Francisco, and I know Xavier was among them and Tiburcio. I am not sure who the others were." He paused with a smile. "If you ask among the people, Father, they will tell you they all were on the expedition. Storytelling is much of what we do, and around this expedition, many stories have been constructed."

Father Juan thought ruefully of what Father Danti had said: *If you are going to believe everything you hear from the Indians in Alta California, Father, you will find your stay very difficult indeed. Pay them no heed.* Here he had an Indian himself telling him the same thing.

"Go on," he encouraged the young man.

"The expedition left and was only gone three or four days when they returned. They had no runaways with them, and Francisco was not with them. The neophytes, though they had been forbidden to talk of what happened, began telling stories of a great battle in the *pantanos*. They said Francisco had been killed, and all of the runaways had escaped."

"They said Francisco was *killed*?" Father Ibarra asked.

"Yes, Father, they said he was killed in the battle with the neophytes." Guillermo paused and thought carefully before speaking again. "Father Danti, though, told a different story. Father Danti said that they had just begun traveling up the marshes of the river when the Indians started getting sick. He said Francisco had gotten sick and died just as they were approaching the runaways. He said there had been no battle but because they stopped to tend to Francisco, the runaways had gotten away. He had decided then that they should return to the mission and would wait until later to continue the pursuit." He paused, apparently at the end of his story. Father Juan continued writing for a few minutes and then looked up at the young man seated across from him.

"You talked to the neophytes who returned, is that not right?"

"Oh yes, we talked then, and for several days later, and in fact we still talk about it. It was a very big event in all of the villages, and among the neophytes at the mission."

"And what do they say?" Father Ibarra persisted. "What do they say about these two stories? How can there be two such different remembrances of one event? For instance, was there a sickness among the Indians on the expedition? Was there a battle between them and the runaways?"

Guillermo fixed the priest with a questioning look. "Father, there is *always* sickness among the Indians. There is sickness among the Indians now. There was sickness among the Indians the day they left, and I am sure it got worse in the marshes of the *San Joaquin*. As to a battle, I think there was a battle. Maybe not what the Spanish soldiers would consider a battle, but I know Father Danti's group and the runaways met. There were muskets and arrows fired."

"Guillermo," the priest began slowly, "I want to ask you to not discuss this conversation we have had with anyone. I myself will seek out Xavier and Tiburcio and talk with them. I will also talk with the soldiers. For now, though, the fewer people talking about this matter, the better. Do you understand?"

"Yes, Father, I fully understand." Guillermo had little more to offer. He stressed that he had not been on the expedition and he was only telling what he had heard.

As the young man left his office, Father Juan sat back and considered what he had heard and what he must do.

Several days later, Father Juan had still not figured out the best way to explore more fully what had happened on that fateful expedition. He was in his office, absentmindedly leafing through some medical journals, when Father Danti stepped in and greeted him.

"*Buenas dias*, Juan. How goes the work? Are you finding any answers to the puzzle of the sickness of the Indians?"

It seemed too good to be true, but Father Danti himself had resolved the problem of how the difficult question of Francisco's death could be visited.

"You know, Antonio," the physician answered, "it continues to be a difficult task. It seems as if the sickness visits mostly the neophytes, and the Indians who live in villages are not so badly affected."

"We have noticed the same thing," Father Danti offered. "We *have* wondered if perhaps the Indians are not as sick as they claim. In the villages, for the most part, they do not have to work. Perhaps those in the mission are only pretending to be sick, so they do not have to work, either."

Father Juan had the register of deaths and burials in front of him. Gesturing to the ledgers, he didn't hesitate to answer. "Pretending to be sick, Antonio, is one thing. Pretending to be dead is entirely another."

The other priest was instantly on his guard. "I am not saying that none of the mission Indians are ever sick," he answered. "I am just saying that not all who claim to be sick, are."

"I am sure that is true," Father Juan answered. "It is also true that it is rare that the Indians in the village are affected by the same diseases which are so devastating to our neophytes. Is it not the case that last winter, on your expedition, the only Indian who got sick and died was one Francisco, a resident of the village, not the mission?"

Now the other priest was quite obviously wary. He literally took a step back.

"What are you saying?" he asked.

"I don't know what I'm saying, Antonio," Father Juan answered genially. "I am just illustrating to you how difficult it is to find answers to the question of what we might do differently to help our converts live better, and longer. Tell me about this Francisco. What was the sickness that killed him?

Was he sick when you left on your expedition? What were his symptoms? What were the symptoms he exhibited in the *pantanos* before he died? Did he have a fever, was he vomiting?"

"I do not know what his symptoms might have been," Father Danti answered curtly. "I do not put my hand on the brow of every Indian who complains about the work we ask them to do. If an *Indio* vomits, he knows to clean it up himself and not to bother me with it. He died and we buried him. If there is one thing we have learned from you physicians it is to quickly bury those who have died, so that their disease will not spread to others. That is what we did. Because some of the others then began complaining of being sick, we returned. The Indians are very good at using the sickness of one to complain of sickness for all. Tell me, Father, why is the sickness and death of this one Indian so important to you?"

Father Juan answered the now obviously agitated friar. "It is not the sickness of this one Indian I am interested in. It is the sickness of all of the Indians. And the sickness of Francisco does not fit the pattern of the others. He did not live in the mission compound. I would assume you would not take an obviously sick Indian on an expedition to the *pantanos*. So, he must have been healthy when you left. Is that not so?" Without giving the other priest time to answer he continued, "And yet, he got sick and died very suddenly. We have found in medicine that it is oftentimes the exception to the rule that points the way to the answer we are seeking. It may be what we call the 'marker,' that will bring to the fore the conditions that prove the rule." He decided to plunge ahead on the course he had set. "I want to see if the death of this Francisco might not be the marker I am seeking."

"I am sure you know what you are doing," the other priest answered icily. "I would not presume to question the judgment of a worldly physician in such matters. I wish you well in your investigation." He turned and, with no farewell, left the office. Father Juan gave a brief sigh and decided that the die had been cast.

It was later that evening, at dinner, that he found just how forcefully it had been thrown. As the monks were finishing their evening meal, Father de Landaeta addressed him.

"Juan, I wonder if you could meet with me for a few minutes after the meal?"

"Yes, Father," he answered. "In your office?"

"My office will do. I'll see you there in a few minutes. Thank you." The superior rose and excused himself. In a few minutes, Father Juan also excused himself to the other friars and walked to the superior's office. He knocked on the door and at the invitation to come in, entered the superior's study. Father de Landaeta sat behind an oak desk reading from a leather-bound volume. A single lantern glowed on the desk. That and a fire burning in the fireplace gave the adobe walls a warm glow.

"Ah, Juan, come in, come in." The superior rose slightly. "Have a seat, please. May I offer you some coffee, or chocolate; perhaps a drop of brandy?" He turned to a credenza along one wall.

"Some chocolate, please," Father Ibarra answered. He settled himself in the chair, briefly glanced at the book-filled shelves and, taking a sip of the chocolate, asked, "What is it I can do for you, Father?"

The superior sipped his own cup thoughtfully and began. "It is about your duties, Father. As we both understand, you are not here as one of the regular mission staff. Your job is to investigate the sickness of the mission Indians and to hopefully find a way we can alleviate that. Would you agree?"

"I would, Father. I think that is a very fair assessment of what I have been sent to do by both the governor of Alta California, and the father president." Again, the mention of the authorities appointing him was deliberate, and again, it had the desired effect. The other priest coughed slightly.

"Well, yes, of course," he said, "and we want to make that task as easy as possible for you. I must tell you though, Father, in all candor, that certain of your lines of inquiry have proven to be disturbing to some of our community."

Father Juan considered carefully how to respond. Taking a deep breath, he answered. "I assume by 'some of our community' you are referring to Father Danti." The older priest looked at him questioningly, and Juan continued, "Father Danti is the only member from among the friars of whom I have made inquiries."

"Yes, Father Danti has indeed spoken to me about your questioning of him. He found it disturbing and, in his words, 'insulting.'"

"Father Superior," Fr. Juan answered, "if I have insulted in any way a brother Franciscan, I will most abjectly apologize. I cannot remember in any way offering any offensive comments to Father Danti. I asked some questions about the death of one of the mission neophytes. It is, after all, the sickness and death of the neophytes I have been sent here to investigate."

"Of course, of course," the superior interjected. "Father Danti just found it perhaps disturbing that the death of this one Indian, who died while under his care, was of so much interest to you."

"Father Danti did express words to that effect to me. I explained to him that Francisco's death was just one of many I was looking at. Since it occurred in a remote location, and since Father Danti was in that same location, I thought he might be able to help me. I further explained to him that Francisco's death did not fit the pattern of so many other deaths, and that was why I was interested in it. Since he was the priest who was with Francisco in his last hours, and he was the priest who buried him, I thought he might have useful information to offer."

The superior nodded slightly. He leaned forward and asked archly, "What is it you understand about Francisco's death?"

Father Ibarra answered. "That he was healthy, and that he left on the expedition, and that he then died on that expedition. That sickness was the cause of his death, yet they had never observed him to be sick." He paused slightly. "I have also received information that *perhaps* he did not die of sickness, but violently."

"And who gave you this last information?"

He thought very briefly of not revealing the source of his information, and then realized that if he was to expect answers to his questions, he must give answers to the questions put to him.

"His widow, Estella. And," he hesitated but continued, "also from Guillermo. I must be clear, Father, that no one has *said* that Francisco died violently. There are just, shall we say, disquieting rumors."

A slight smugness crossed the superior's face.

"We have heard those rumors, Juan. We have tried to discourage them, but they persist. They have no basis in fact." He continued. "Did you know that there is an intense personal relationship between Guillermo and Estella? Their conduct since the death of her husband borders on scandalous."

Father Juan felt a decided sense of deflation. The other priest continued.

"Guillermo wants to take Estella as his wife. Estella, if her husband was killed in the service of the Spanish military, would be entitled to a small pension. Such a lifetime benefit would be a very attractive dowry to the Indians. Thus, the story of a battle, and the death of Francisco at the hands of the runaways." The superior leaned back in his chair.

"I knew of none of this," Father Ibarra mumbled. It had never occurred to him that the two sources of the story might have a common origin.

"I suggest, Father," Father Landaeta continued, "that you give some credence to those who have been dealing with these people for much longer than you have. I realize that you are charged with a particular duty, and that you are eager to fulfill that duty. But you must keep in mind that you are not dealing with the privileged classes of Europe, nor even of Mexico. These people do not see things the same way we do and their view of truth is different than ours."

A somewhat chastened Father Juan responded. "You have given me information I did not have, Father, and I appreciate it. I will consider it carefully and take it in to consideration, in my future queries."

"Good. I think you should." The superior raised one eyebrow. "There will be future queries?"

"Yes, Father; I think there must be. Perhaps just a few. If I may, in fact, a question of you?

"Yes?" the other answered warily.

"You have said that Father Danti feels I am overly concerned about the death of this one Indian, is that correct?"

"Yes, that is correct." The superior answered with some hesitation.

"Well, Father, I put a similar question to you." At the older man's questioning look he continued. "Why is Father Danti so overly concerned about the death of this one Indian?"

It was the very next day when Father Juan was made to realize just how concerned Father Danti—and indeed, probably Father Landaeta—were about the death of "this one Indian." He had been working in his office for several hours, trying to bring order to his notes, when he realized that Guillermo had not come in. He consulted his watch and saw that it was ten-thirty. He went to the door and called to a neophyte who was tending some plantings in the cemetery. When the young man came over, he asked him, "Have you seen Guillermo? Could you check in the quarters and see if he is ill?"

The Indian examined the priest's face intently.

"Guillermo, Father? Guillermo has gone to Monterey."

"Monterey?" the priest asked, in total confusion. "Why has he gone to Monterey? *How* has he gone to Monterey? Monterey is over three days away. Why has he gone to Monterey?" he asked again.

"I do not know, Father." The Indian began backing away. "I do not know. Father Landaeta had him go with some soldiers and with Father Cruzado, who left for Monterey this morning. I do not know anything else. *Buenas dias, Padre.*" The man turned and walked away, and a thoroughly confused and thoroughly troubled Father Juan once more made the trip to the superior's office.

"*Buenas dias, Juan.*" Father de Landaeta greeted him. "What can I do for you?"

"I have just been told that Guillermo has been sent to Monterey."

"That is true," the superior answered. "I am sorry that I did not have the opportunity to let you know. It was decided at the last minute that he should join Father Cruzado, who has been recalled by the father president. I will find you another assistant as soon as possible."

"It is not the loss of an assistant I am concerned about, Father. It is what seems like the precipitous transfer of an Indian who was providing me information helpful to my investigation."

The superior studied the monk importuning him. "If I understood you correctly the other day, Father, Guillermo has provided you with all the information he had on the matter you are investigating. Which information, I must remind you, was second-hand at best. As we have previously discussed, Guillermo is being considered for membership in our order. All candidates for ordination must receive the approval of the father president. Since Father Cruzado was scheduled to go to Monterey, it was decided that now might be a good time for Guillermo to undergo that scrutiny."

Father Juan decided that further objection would be fruitless. He knew very well that the lives of the neophytes were lived entirely at the whim of the mission superiors. Quite often they were sent from one mission to another, as the needs of the Franciscans dictated, and with absolutely no consideration of the needs of the Indians.

"I understand, Father," he demurred. "I hope he will do well in his new home." He excused himself and returned to his office. He spent most of the afternoon contemplating this new complication. Finally, he decided that it was true that Father de Landaeta's view of what Guillermo had offered was correct. Guillermo had told him the story, as he understood it, of what had happened on the expedition. To that narrative he would have nothing more to add. With this basic information to work with, it was up to him to proceed. That evening as the meal was concluding, he announced those plans for proceeding. "I am going to take a walk this evening, and explore some of the mission environs. I will probably not be back until Vespers."

Without waiting for any questions or remonstrance, he excused himself and left the refectory. He went to his cell and took a small lantern and a heavier cowl to wear. He walked from the mission compound and headed towards the *presidio* and the waterfront. Halfway to the *presidio*, he turned to the south and made his way to the Indian village. He arrived at the village just as the sun was setting, and the evening fog was rolling in through the mouth of the bay.

The village was a collection of mud and reed huts built in an irregular circle. The center of the village was flanked with the homes of the older, senior members of the clan. It was a gathering place where the village members met to socialize and discuss matters of importance. In successive circles around this central area, newer members of the village had built their huts. It was the center of the village to which Father Juan headed, where several old men and a few children were gathered. The men were seated around a large fire, and the children were playing in and out of the shadows. There were no women. As he approached the group, one of the men stood and greeted him.

"*Buenas tardes, Padre.* What is it you need?"

"I am Father Juan Ibarra," he introduced himself. "I would like to visit with you for a while."

"You are the priest doctor, am I not correct?" the man asked. "You are visiting San Francisco but you do not belong to the mission."

"Yes, that is correct," Father Juan answered. "I have been at the mission for some time now, but I have never had the opportunity to visit you."

"You are welcome, Father; have a seat." He gestured to a log, flattened on one side, one of several arranged around the fire pit. He turned to one of the staring boys standing at the edge of the group. He said something to him in the native tongue, and the boy ran off to one of the nearby huts. The boy had a brief conversation with a woman tending an outdoor oven and gestured back to the group of men at the fire. She glanced at the group and turned to a pot on the stove, filling a cup that she handed to the boy. He came back to the group of men and handed it to the man, who turned and offered it to the still-standing priest.

"Chocolate, Father," he said, and gestured once more to the log. "Have a seat, Father. Have a seat, visit with us."

Father Juan took the steaming cup, gathered his robes about him and sat on the log. The man introduced himself as Claudio, the *alcalde* of the village. Claudio introduced the other men around the fire, although their names were lost on the priest who was still puzzling in his own mind where the conversation would go from there. The talk initially was stilted and cautious. There were comments about the weather, questions of how he was finding San Francisco, some shared jokes in their own tongue and cautious laughter. A visit from one of the Franciscans to the village was apparently a rare occasion. In fact, for quite a period of time the conversation among the Indians devolved into a heated discussion centered on *when* exactly a priest *had* visited the village last. There seemed to be two schools of thought. One group maintained it was over a year ago, when Father Cambon had come to deliver the last rites to an elderly lady dying of the "spotted disease." A minority held steadfast that it had been when Father Danti had come to recruit members for his expedition.

Seeing perhaps an opportunity, Father Juan interjected. "Actually, it is that expedition that I would like to visit with you about."

This comment threw a decided pall over the group. Some of the men who had begun to relax literally sat more upright. Several pulled their cloaks more tightly around themselves. They looked, without exception, to Claudio.

"Oh, Father," Claudio answered warily, "we do not know anything about that. Father Danti, when he was looking for members of the expedition, was looking for young men. Not old men like us." Several of the men laughed, and there were several nods of affirmation.

Father Juan plunged ahead. "But I understand that there was at least one villager who went on that expedition."

"And who never came back," one of the men muttered, receiving a disapproving glare from Claudio.

"Yes, yes," Father Juan offered, "that man was Francisco, I understand. His wife—or I should say his widow—is still here, is she not? Estella, is that not her name? Perhaps I could visit with Estella?"

All of the men in the circle stared at Claudio. Fr. Juan could appreciate the position that *alcalde* was in. His was a position of authority and responsibility. It was also a position granted only by the good graces of the father superior. All of the villages in the immediate area of a mission were very decidedly under the authority of that particular mission. Their lives were not as stringently controlled by the Franciscans as those who lived on mission grounds, but their limited freedom was certainly at the forbearance of the Franciscans. The subject of Francisco's death had been a topic of very heated conversation ever since the expedition had returned. The father superior had made it clear to Claudio that any dispute about the account Father Danti had given was disobedience and an unlawful challenge to authority, bordering on rebellion. Father de Landaeta impressed Claudio with the understanding that his position as *alcalde* was dependent on his suppression of such talk. Now, he was faced with one of the Franciscans who was asking to visit the story again. He called the young boy back and spoke to him briefly. The boy turned and ran off to the huts.

"We will have you talk to Estella, Father," Claudio explained. Father Juan turned back to his cup of rapidly cooling chocolate. The men around the fire sat in stolid silence, each waiting to see what would develop next. They did not have to wait long. The young boy came back to the group with a woman, perhaps slightly older than Estella, in tow.

"This is Oralia, Father," Claudio explained. "She will take you to visit Estella." At the priest's questioning glance, he explained. "It would not do to have a Franciscan visit with a young woman without a chaperone, no?" The priest smiled, not at all prepared to argue with the logic, and stood to follow Oralia. They walked through the village, to one of the outer rings. During the brief trip, Father Juan found that Oralia was no more a conversationalist than any of the natives he had met. Brief, one-word replies were all he got in response to the few perfunctory questions he asked on the short walk. Arriving at one of the huts, Oralia motioned to the priest to wait outside.

"Estella," she called, and, pushing aside the deerskin covering on the door, went into the hut. As he waited, Father Juan glanced around the village. All of the huts had outdoor ovens, and at several of these he noticed groups of people. Lantern glow showed through all of the buildings and between the settling fog and setting sun, darkness was descending on the village. Very shortly, Oralia came out and beckoned him inside.

He glanced around the small enclosure. Several rugs were scattered around a packed earth floor. There were baskets and containers scattered about. Along one wall, a small pallet was covered with reeds and blankets. Next to it, the infant lay sleeping bound in blankets on top of a mattress of reeds. Estella, who had been sitting on some scattered rugs, stood as he entered. She put down some sewing she had been working on and greeted him.

"*Buenas tarde, Padre.* Please come in, have a seat." She spoke a few words in her own tongue to Oralia, who stepped back through the door. Father Juan settled himself on a pile of rugs and furs that Estella gestured to. She was not wearing the simple garb of the neophytes, but had on a more flowing gown, decorated with colorful symbols, whose significance he could only guess at. The dress had a modest curved neckline and he could see a plain silver chain disappearing into the material. Her short hair was held back from her face with two abalone shell clasps.

"*Buenas tardes, Estella.* Can we visit?"

"Of course, Father. I am happy to see you here, although I must tell you that not many of the others are."

"Why is that, my dear?"

"It is not often that the Franciscans come to our village, Father, and usually, when they do, they do not bring good news."

"Ah," the priest answered, "that is what I have come to discuss. The unhappy news the Franciscans brought the last time they visited, which I understand was when they came to ask Francisco to go on the expedition."

Estella responded without hesitation. "They did not *ask* Francisco go on the expedition Father. They *told* him that he was going on the expedition the next day."

"Ah, yes..." Father Juan began, when he was interrupted by Oralia returning to the hut. She was carrying a pot of steaming herbal tea and two cups. She poured one for Father Ibarra and one for Estella. She took none herself, and without a word sat down on another set of rugs. Father Juan took a sip of the tea and, glancing hesitantly at Oralia, began again.

"I was, uh, hoping to visit with you some more..." his voice trailed off.

Estella interrupted him. "Oralia is my very best friend." She smiled slightly. "She is here only to see that my virtue is not compromised. Until I find a suitable husband, the village will look very carefully to my wellbeing. Oralia and I have been friends since childhood. She did not abandon our friendship when I became a Catholic, and believe me, that is unusual among our people. She assisted me when my baby was born. She is a widow like me," here her voice dropped, "although, unlike me, she has lost a child as well as a husband. It was one of the spotted diseases. Nothing that you and I discuss tonight will ever be repeated by Oralia. Please tell me what it is that you wish to speak about."

Since she had a least indirectly brought up one question he needed answered, Father Juan asked, "I have been told, Estella, that there is a relationship between you and Guillermo. Is that true?"

Estella took a swallow of her tea and smiled as she answered. "The Franciscans worry too much about what young people might be doing. If they even see a young man and a young woman just talking, they think they are sinning." She added reflectively, "For people who have nothing to do with women, you priests worry an awful lot about what women might be doing." She went on, "Guillermo would like there to be a relationship between us, Father. He is an unattached young man, and I am now an unattached young lady. He has been very attentive to me since my husband died. As I said before, it is a tradition of our people that a woman who has lost her husband be cared for. It is not unusual among our people that a woman who has lost her husband will be chosen by another man very quickly. But in the case you are concerned about, there are about three things that make such a happening between Guillermo and me impossible."

"And they are?"

"Guillermo and I are both Catholics. We cannot marry without the priest's permission. Do you think that is likely to happen?" Without waiting for his answer, she continued. "Also, Father, although Guillermo is a very nice young man, and very helpful to me, I am not at all attracted to him. I think the other priests may be right: his future is with the Franciscans, and not with me as his wife." Estella was now smiling with a decided air of satisfaction.

"The third thing?" Father Juan asked. "What is the third thing which you say makes a relationship between you and Guillermo impossible?"

"The third thing, Father ..." and now the smile was gone. She looked at the priest with the same intense stare she had given to close their last visit. "The third thing is that until I find out for sure what happened to my Francisco, until I am able to honor him and bury him in holy ground, there will be no man for me. Not chosen by my people, nor the Franciscans, nor by myself. The relationship between Guillermo and me is that of an Ohlone man protecting an Ohlone woman, and I hope it continues."

Father Juan could not hold himself back. "Guillermo is gone," he said, "he has been sent to Monterey."

"I know that, Father," she answered.

"You do?" he asked. "He just left this morning."

"Father," Estella answered disarmingly, "there is nothing the Spanish do that is not immediately known by all of the people. We are present at everything you do. We prepare your meals and serve your food, we clean your rooms. We tend your gardens and your animals. We see and know everything you do. I was told of Guillermo being sent to Monterey probably before he crossed the first hill to the south. I am sorry if I was the reason he was sent to Monterey. I know he cares for me, and perhaps, without realizing it, the Franciscans have done us both a favor by sending him away. As I have said, I do not have the feelings for him that I think he has for me. Perhaps his time in Monterey will help him to realize we were not meant for each other."

Father Juan leaned back on his cushions and considered the lady in front of him. *How old is she?* he wondered. *Seventeen, eighteen, fourteen?* He had no idea. She had the face and body of a child. She had shown herself, though, to be a determined and forceful woman. She was a mother, and she was a widow. *Age,* he mused, *is not a matter of years.*

"Estella, I know that your husband's death would have to be very disturbing to you. It is not just his dying that brought you to me. There is something more than Francisco's death. What is it?"

"I cannot say for sure, Father. I want to be very careful in this. I have heard some of the people who were on that expedition say they don't think Francisco was sick. They don't think he died of a sickness."

Father Juan decided that this guarded conversation was not

accomplishing anything. "I have heard it said that Francisco was *killed*. Perhaps in a battle with the runaways. Is that what you think?"

Estella nodded slowly and slightly.

"Why would anyone want to hide that, Estella? If Francisco was killed in a battle, why wouldn't they just have said that?"

Estella slowly shook her head. "I don't know for sure, Father. Because questions would be asked? Because they would have to explain why the soldiers were fighting with the runaways when they were not supposed to be pursuing them at all? I don't know, Father."

"Estella," Father Juan explained, "I am going to investigate very thoroughly Francisco's death. There are enough unusual facts as I understand them to necessitate that. I will be very honest with everything I find out about it. You must give me time and you must trust me. I will tell you nothing but the truth of what I uncover." He rose to leave. "Thank you, Estella," he said, "for visiting with me. You have given me more to think about. As I promised you, I am looking very carefully at Francisco's death. I will not cease to do that until I, and I hope you, are satisfied with what I have found. *Buenas noches*."

"*Buenas noches, Padre*," she answered warmly, "and thank you for coming to visit, and thank you for what you are doing. I know it is not an easy thing, to go against the wishes of your people, and I know it is the wishes of the Spanish that this awful event be forgotten."

Oralia stood, said a few words to Estella, and led the priest from the hut.

As he started out from the village, he stopped by the central fire to get a light for his lantern. It was now not only fully dark but foggy. Claudio insisted on sending a young man back with him to the mission.

"It is not far to the mission, Father, but it is very dark. Once you are away from the lights of the village, all of the hills will look the same to you. You could end up in the bay. Magno will get you back to the mission and he will be back here before you are in your bed. *Buenas noches, Padre*."

Father Juan spent the next several days trying to figure a way to breach the impenetrable wall of silence that surrounded the death of Francisco. Fathers Danti and de Landaeta dismissed as "preposterous" any suggestion that anything untoward had taken place on that ill-fated expedition. The lives of the Indians were so rigidly controlled that he had no hope of approaching any of them without that information getting immediately back to the other priests. And so, it occurred to him, perhaps the best way to examine the issue was to simply do what he had been sent to San Francisco to do. A studied examination of the diseases that so plagued the mission would give him an opportunity to talk in some detail, and on his own terms, with the entire population of Mission San Francisco: priests, Indians and soldiers alike. No one could object to that.

He began a careful examination of the mission records, the birth and death registers, and the superior's own journals. He soon discovered that virtually every one of the mission neophytes had at one time or another been infected with some serious illness. He carefully noted names whenever they were recorded. He was surprised to find that Father De Landaeta himself had been bedridden for several days with fevers, chills and delirious ramblings, more than a year ago.

After a week of methodically plodding through records of sickness and death, he had a list of names of people he would like to interview further. Of particular interest on that list were the names of Estella, Xavier, Tiburcio, and Father de Landaeta himself. One evening at supper, he approached Father de Landaeta.

"I think I have the names of all of the neophytes who have survived serious illness." He paused to give his next comment what he hoped would be a casual indifference. "I will soon begin interviewing those people to get their own thoughts on their illness and its course. I hope that will give me some information on common characteristics I might explore."

The superior nodded approvingly. Father Danti interrupted.

"I hope that will not interfere with their work schedules. We are behind on our production of cloth, and some of the merchants in town have begun suggesting that perhaps it is time to begin trading with the Russian and British ships that are increasingly appearing in the harbor. The commander of the *presidio*, and indeed the governor himself, are distressed at such a prospect."

"No, no," Father Juan assured him. "I would have just a few questions to ask. I can easily do that at the end of the workday when they are headed back to their quarters or their villages."

"If you are going to talk with every *Indio* who has ever been sick," Father Danti interjected, "you are going to talk with every *Indio* in Alta California. Sickness is their answer to a request to work."

Father Juan answered carefully, and, he hoped, lightly.

"I know what you are saying, Antonio. It is for that reason that I will make my list of only those who were sick enough to keep bedridden for more than three days. Those seem to be the illnesses that cause the most problem at Mission San Francisco." He turned back to Father Landaeta. "In fact, Father, you are on that list. I note that you were sick for several weeks over a year ago. I think it might be helpful to me if I could interview you about that illness."

The superior nodded. "I certainly remember at least parts of it. I was very sick for many days, and of several of those days I have no memory at all. In fact, from time to time I fall ill with the same symptoms, but never as bad as that first episode. I will be happy to give you whatever information you seek regarding that."

Father Juan continued. "When I am ready to begin interviewing the Indians, I could each day give you a list of those I wish to speak with, and you could instruct them to report to my office as they are dismissed from work. It would probably only be two or three a day. My interview of you can wait until a time when it is convenient for you."

The superior considered the suggestion. "That would be fine, Father. I think that would be a good approach. Let me know when you are ready to begin interviewing the neophytes and I will let you know when I have some free time to give you for an interview of me."

"*Bueno, bueno,*" Father Juan answered, forcing himself to sound mildly disinterested. "I will let you know, Father."

What he wouldn't let Father de Landaeta know was that in the course of those interviews, he would have the opportunity to visit on the matter of the expedition with those who might have some knowledge of it. He knew that he would have to proceed cautiously, but he felt confident that he was finally proceeding.

He waited several days, to let the idea of his interviewing various of the neophytes lose its novelty, before he actually began the process. Finally, he sent Father de Landaeta a list of three names—two elderly women and a twelve-year-old child—and asked if they could report to his office when their duties for the day were done.

The young man appeared first, obviously full of trepidation and wonderment as to why he had been called. He was easily put at ease by Father Juan's smiling demeanor and the offer of a cup of chocolate. The priest explained to him what he was trying to accomplish, and why he wanted to talk with him. The young man eagerly jumped into the process. He told Father Juan that they shared the same name, although, as he explained with great seriousness, "I am called Juanito. My father is Juan."

Juanito worked as a helper in the kitchen, fetching food and cooking implements for the cooks, and cleaning up after the meal. His father was a *vaquero* with the mission herds and when he was bigger, he would be a *vaquero* as well.

"The *vaqueros* can ride horses," he explained with awe. "No other *Indios* are allowed to ride." When Father Juan complimented him on his Spanish, he looked slightly perplexed, and commented, "It is my language, *Padre*." The monk had to remind himself that of course, for one so young, that would have been the only language he was allowed to speak and the language he would have heard since his birth. He asked him about his mother.

"My mother is dead, *Padre*. She died of the spotted disease at the same time I was sick with it." He added solemnly, "I did not die of it." Father Juan asked him about his sickness. When had it come, how long had he been ill, what did he feel like, how long before he started to feel better? The child was a poor historian. He remembered spots on his face and arms, and even in his ears. He had been hot and had a cough. His eyes were sore. The timeline of any of these he did not know.

"There were many people sick then, Father. My mother was sick, but my father was not."

Father Juan thanked the young man, offered him a sweet, and sent him on his way. Watching the young boy leave, Father Juan saw him stopped by two old ladies who questioned him briefly, and then made their own way to the priest's tiny office. He spent the same first few minutes trying to put them at ease and explaining to them what he was trying to accomplish. Their stories were essentially the same as young Juanito's. They had no clear idea when they had been sick. When Father Juan prompted them from his records, they readily agreed with whatever dates he suggested. They had been sick along with lots of the other neophytes. Some got better, some died. When he asked them why they thought some had died and some had gotten better, they simply shrugged.

This type of interview continued for several weeks with a wide variety of the mission population, and with generally unremarkable results. Except for an occasional reference to a plant they had taken, or a cure applied by a native healer, the stories were depressingly similar: "I got sick, I was confined to the quarters for several days, I got better. Others were sick, others died." There were distressingly frequent references to punishments inflicted; often, as far as he could tell, just for getting sick.

Finally, he decided the time had come to move to the next step of his search. He sent Father de Landaeta a request with the usual three names on it. One of the names this time was Xavier. He included with this list a personal request to Father de Landaeta: When would be a good time for the father superior to be interviewed? Would the father superior agree to being interviewed, so that Father Juan could include his illness in the histories he was compiling? The immediate answer from the superior was to agree without hesitation to be interviewed "at Father Juan's convenience."

The two Indians he had requested appeared at the end of the very next workday. Father Juan spoke to the first along the same lines as he had conducted the other interviews, with much the same results. As he completed the "routine" questions with Xavier, he cautiously shifted the topic.

"If I may, Xavier, I would like to ask you a few more questions."

"Yes, Father?" the Indian answered.

"I understand, Xavier, that you were on the expedition where Francisco died."

Xavier said nothing, but nodded slightly. Father Juan studied the man in front of him. Xavier was young, perhaps only twenty-five or so. He appeared strong, and healthy. His answers to the priest's questions had been clear and unambiguous. Unlike many of the others, he seemed sure of dates and times, and had described with unusual clarity the symptoms of his disease. While polite and respectful to the priest, he did not seem cowed nor unduly deferential. There was no doubt that a certain reserve had overtaken him now. He considered Father Juan for so long that the monk felt compelled to add, "I think you know, Xavier, that while I am a member of the Franciscan order, I am not part of Mission San Francisco. I have been sent here by the governor to see if I can find out why so many Indians at Mission San Francisco are dying. One of the Indians who has died was Francisco. It is reported that he died of a disease. It has also been reported that he was not sick. It is my job to answer questions about his death."

With no change in his expression, Xavier began. "You know of course, Father, that I am a Christian neophyte of this mission." As the priest nodded, he continued. "I am a young man, and I believe that for now my life is tied to Mission San Francisco. I have plans, though, that do not involve the mission. Under the mission fathers, I have become a skilled mason. The town of Yerba Buena is growing. My skills will be much needed in that town, and I intend to use them to give me a life away from the mission. For now, though, my life is at the mission. As I prepare to build a different life away from the mission, I will need the recommendation of the mission fathers to do that. In fact, I will need the *permission* of the mission fathers to do that. I do not want to be sent away as Guillermo was."

Father Juan felt compelled to interject. "I promise you, Xavier, that nothing you tell me will be used in any way other than in finding out how Francisco died and why there are so many neophyte deaths at San Francisco." Here he paused significantly. "I must tell you in all honesty that some of the things you tell me may go in a report I will send to the father president and to the governor in Monterey."

Xavier looked at monk intently. "Estella told me that she has spoken to you. I know of the questions Estella has about Francisco's death."

At the mention of Estella's name Father Juan decided that he had better get one inevitable question answered. "What is your relationship to Estella?" he asked.

Without hesitation the young man answered. "Estella was the wife of my very good friend. Often when I was tired of the mission routine or meals, I would visit them in the village and they would entertain me in their home. I am godfather to their child. Estella is now the widow of my very good friend and I will help her and protect her in any way I can." He added with a questioning note, "Our relationship may be different in the future. I do not know. As I have told you, I plan to have a new life away from the mission. Perhaps Estella might be part of that life; she is young, she is pretty and she is a good friend." He shrugged slightly. "One of the first things we were taught as neophytes is that it is a sin to tell a lie. Ask me what you need to know, Father, and I will tell you."

Father Juan began. "When you left on the expedition was Francisco sick?"

"No, Father, Francisco was never sick."

"Did he get sick while you were on the expedition?"

"No, Father."

"Not even in the marshes of the *San Joaquin*?"

"No, Father."

"When did you last see Francisco?"

"On the morning we spotted the runaways."

"How was he then?"

"He was fine, Father. We talked just before we set out on that day's march."

"Did you see Francisco's body after he had died?"

"No, Father, the soldiers and the priest had buried him."

"Tell me what happened that day."

The young man gave a slight sigh. "It was on the second day of the expedition. We had camped for the night. That morning we got up and began marching again. As the day wore on, the soldiers said that we should not march in a large group, and that we should not talk. We would make too much noise and the runaways would hear us. We should march close enough to see each other but not close enough to talk. They divided us into two groups about a league apart. The first group was all Indians. I was in that group. We were to watch for the runaways and if we spotted them, we were to keep them in sight and send a messenger back to the second group. The second group was Father Danti, the soldiers and one Indian—Francisco." He paused briefly to recall. "I don't suppose, Father, you have ever tried to march through the *pantanos*. It is hard work and it is hard to maintain any sort of order. In a very short time, not only were the two groups widely separated, but each group would find themselves either walking up the back of their companions, or losing sight of them.

"Late that morning we spotted the runaways. We sent one man back to tell the soldiers, and we tried to keep the runaways in sight while we waited for the soldiers to come up." Here he shook his head ruefully. "We were excited that we had found the runaways so quickly. When people get excited, they get noisy. The runaways heard us and began going all different ways into the swamps. We tried to run after them, and it was then things got very confused. Everyone started shouting, the runaways started throwing rocks and shooting arrows at us, and some of the soldiers came running up. Corporal Montoya, Father Danti, Francisco and some of the other soldiers were a little further back. I am not sure what happened next; some gunshots were fired, I don't know how many. Those of us in front of the soldiers laid down in the reeds. We were afraid of being shot by the soldiers behind us. More gunshots were fired as we lay there; then suddenly all was quiet. The runaways had completely disappeared. We lay in the reeds for a long time, and finally I raised my head up to see what was happening. Shortly behind me were some soldiers. Further back was Father Danti, with more soldiers. I stood up and began to walk back to them, and they shouted to me to stop. Father Danti shouted to all of us, 'Stay there, do not come back. Watch the runaways, go after the runaways.' I tried to tell him that the runaways were gone, but he just shouted more. He called me an ignorant savage, and told me that we were letting them get away. 'Go after them, go after them,' he shouted. My companions were now all standing, and they asked me what we should do. 'They don't understand,' I said, 'I'll go tell them.' I started walking back again, and one of the soldiers fired his musket at me. I heard the ball whistle past my head. 'Go after them, go after them,' Father Danti screamed. 'We will catch up to you shortly. Go after them.'

"Well, Father," Xavier continued, "I don't know if you have ever heard a musket ball go by your head, but once you have, it is not a sound you ever want to hear again. I told my companions that we should go, and we started off in a direction away from Father Danti. We knew the runaways would shoot arrows at us, so we walked off toward the side. We knew that they were armed, and that they would fight. None of us had weapons. We did not want to meet them again. We just wanted to get away from that crazy Father Danti. We started walking in the general direction the runaways had gone."

He looked intently at the priest to see if his editorial comment had been ill received. There was no indication on the part of Father Juan that he had even heard it. He simply asked, "Were any of the runaways hit by the soldier's fire?"

"I don't know, Father. I know that they disappeared in the *pantanos*, when the shots were fired, but whether that was because they were shot, or they were just hiding in the grass as we were, I don't know.

"We continued for at least two hours. Finally, we heard noises in the reeds behind us. A soldier came up to us. He was one of the youngest ones. He had been running to catch up to us. He was out of breath and could hardly talk.

'It is time to go back,' he gasped. We began discussing, in our own language, about whether we *should* go back. Some wanted to keep going and join our brothers who had run away. They wanted to keep going and leave the soldiers and Father Danti. Tiburcio even suggested that we should kill the soldier and take his gun. Several of us, though, had wives or families back at the mission, and it was finally decided that we would go back. We followed the soldier back to the other group. We reached them just as it was growing dark. They were camped close to where we had camped the first day.

"Father Danti was still angry. 'You let them get away. You are all, stupid, ignorant savages. You let them get away.' I know better than to ever talk with Father Danti when he is angry. He has had neophytes flogged because they did not bow low enough in his presence. The soldiers were silent and angry-looking. As I began to move back with my companions I asked, 'Where is Francisco?'"

"Father Danti shouted at me. 'Francisco is dead. He died of a sickness this morning and we buried him so his disease would not spread.' The soldiers said nothing. We camped for the night and the next day returned to the mission."

Xavier gave a deep sigh and finished, "That is what I know, Father."

Father Juan completed the entry in his journal, sat back and looked at the young man. Xavier, for his part, sat motionless in his chair. Finally, Father Juan spoke.

"What about Tiburcio? He was on the expedition, too. What would he have to tell me?"

"Tiburcio was farther forward than I was. He may know more about what the runaways were doing and how they fired back at us. He will not know anything more about what was taking place behind us. Only Father Danti and the soldiers will know about that. I do not talk to the soldiers at all, and I try not to talk to Father Danti any more than I have to. You must realize if you talk to Tiburcio that he always wants to impress people. He will tell you what he thinks you want to hear. He will put himself in a much more important role than he had."

"How has Father Danti been since you got back from the expedition?"

Xavier shrugged. "He has been Father Danti. He is an unhappy and angry man. He does not like the Indians and he treats us all with anger. He punishes frequently. He is known among the people as 'Sergeant Danti.'" At the priest's questioning glance, he explained. "He is always striding about shouting orders. He is more like one of the sergeants than one of the priests."

Father Juan concluded the interview. "Xavier, it is important for now that this must be only between you and me."

"I understand, Padre. *Buenas noches.*"

That night at supper, Father de Landaeta brought up Father Juan's earlier request to talk to him about the illness that had disabled him some time ago.

"You wanted to talk with me, Juan, about my illness last year?"

"Yes, Father, when it is convenient for you."

"Come to my study and we will visit now."

Father Ibarra excused himself from the table and followed the superior to his office. Father de Landaeta seemed relaxed and pleasant. He offered the other priest the inevitable cup of chocolate, and even went so far as to suggest a dollop of brandy in it. As the two men sipped their drinks, the superior assured Father Juan that he would take no offense if the physician made notes during their conversation.

"I understand, Juan, that it is your job to gather information on diseases here at Mission San Francisco, and to prepare a report to the father president."

Father Juan surveyed the older priest, and in particular his pock-marked face. He made what he hoped was a surreptitious note in the journal he held: *From the scars on his face it is obvious that Father de Landaeta is a survivor of smallpox as a child.*

"What is it you wish to know about my illness, Juan?" the other priest asked.

"It would be helpful, Father, if you could tell me what you remember about your illness."

The superior smiled slightly. "I don't have to remember very far back, for while the worst of the illness was over a year ago, I am still visited with it today. It comes back at odd intervals, but never as bad as it was last fall.

"Tell me about that, please."

"The illness when I had it last year was a series of body aches, headaches, fever and chills. I still, from time to time, am visited with those same symptoms, although not as intensely."

"Were any of the Indians sick at the same time?"

"Father," the superior intoned, "the Indians are *always* sick." Father Juan remembered the uncannily similar phrase Guillermo had used. The older priest continued. "So yes, some of the Indians were sick at the same time, but their symptoms were not entirely the same as mine; they had fevers and body aches, but I believe no chills and no headaches. They had spots on their bodies which I never developed. I have been told that if you have one of the spotted diseases as a child you may get it again as an adult, only you will not have the spots. I think that is what I had." Father Juan took detailed notes.

They continued their question and answer session well into the evening. The superior seemed genuinely interested in providing detailed answers. Father Juan discovered a slightly more human Father de Landaeta than he had seen before. He remained aloof, as was befitting his position, but an occasional hint of humor sneaked through when he was discussing his helplessness and the attempts of the other friars to succor him.

"Brother Anzar was an excellent nurse; he has missed his calling. Father Danti could barely bring himself to visit my bed, and when he did, he couldn't leave fast enough. Guadalupe, one of the neophytes, acted like my mother, not just in caring for me but in shooing away visitors at my more difficult times. It was a very unpleasant illness, Father, and each time I have a new attack of it, I fear it is going to be like that first time—but so far, it has never developed into that unpleasantness. Guadalupe gives me a very bitter tea to drink, which I take to please her. She claims it is that tea that keeps me from getting sicker. I don't believe that, but I offer up the horrible taste of that brew for the poor souls in purgatory, and she smiles when I drink it." Father Juan made a particular note to talk with Guadalupe further.

The evening was turning to night when he rose and excused himself from the superior. *"Buenas noches, Padre,"* he said. "This has been a most interesting talk. You have given me much to consider further. I don't mind telling you that my many talks with the Indians have not been as helpful as this one talk with you. They do not, or do not *want*, to remember the details of their illnesses as well as you do. When I have studied my findings more carefully, I will give you a report."

"They are an ignorant people," the other priest said, and then added with genuine warmth, "but God loves them, and it has fallen to us to educate them as to that love."

Father Juan felt compelled to answer. "You know, Father, I have found them to be a people with a very firm grasp on their own view of the world. Those who do convert, though, have a strong allegiance to the faith we have brought them."

Father de Landaeta rubbed his face and answered tiredly. "You are right, of course, Juan. I have found much satisfaction in our work here. In fact, if I could work only with the *Indios* I would find it more satisfying. Unfortunately," he sighed, running his hand over his face again, "as the superior of the mission, I must attend to many administrative details, and I must deal with the failings of not only the *Indios* but of the soldiers as well, and perhaps, most difficult of all," he paused very briefly, "of the members of our order. *Buenas noches, Juan,* I look forward to your findings."

11

Several weeks later, Father Juan was still engaged in his dual task: chronicling the history of diseases among the native population of the mission, while trying to gain as much information as possible about the ill-fated expedition to recover some runaways a year earlier. He continued with his examination of the survivors of various diseases at Mission San Francisco. The stories were depressingly similar and generally uninformative.

His interview of Tiburcio had proved true to Xavier's prediction. Tiburcio claimed that he had been chosen for the expedition because "he would know where the runaways had gone." Tiburcio, it seemed, had run away himself, only to be caught and returned. Tiburcio was more than willing to offer great detail about what had transpired on the day they discovered the runaways. His answers were long and rambling and full of vivid descriptors: "many runaways," "the missiles darkened the sky," "I ran after them bravely." Father Juan found himself constantly bringing the man back to the question that had been asked, and trying to slow down his rapid narrative. Careful questioning ultimately uncovered the fact that in fact, the Indian had been further from the events in question than had Xavier. It was clear to Father Juan that Tiburcio's recitation was some combination of information he had gotten from others of the expedition, and an embellishment of Xavier's story.

However, Tiburcio, as one of the most far-forward of the Indians, did offer one thing of which he was sure: The runaways had launched only arrows, spears, and rocks at their pursuers. They had no firearms. He also gave Father Juan the names of some of the soldiers who had been on the expedition. There was Corporal Montoya in charge, and Privates Melendez, Lopez and Galindo. He wasn't sure how many soldiers there were: "Maybe six or eight." It had been Private Galindo who had caught up with their party and told them to turn back to join the others. Tiburcio made no mention of any suggestion that they might kill the private, take his gun and join the runaways.

As interesting as his interviews with Indians were, it was Father de Landaeta's illness that proved to be one of the more rewarding he had unearthed. He had spoken with Guadalupe about the unpleasant concoction she continued to give Father de Landaeta at his slightest complaint of a headache. Guadalupe told him it was made from the bark of tree which grew "far away; yes, maybe Mexico," in answer to his question. He remembered reading as a student in Madrid that the Jesuits in Peru had for more than one hundred years been sending to Rome a powder made from the bark of the *cinchona* tree. It proved to be very efficacious in treating the malaria that had plagued Rome for hundreds of years. Reviewing Father de Landaeta's description of his symptoms, he found them to be a textbook example of malaria, particularly the reoccurrences.

Malaria was a disease Father Juan had always associated with equatorial climes, and the damp chilly weather of San Francisco was as far from equatorial as he could imagine. None of the Indians had ever heard of a tree named *cinchona*; Guadalupe knew only that the tree grew "far away." She had gotten the powder from one of the neophytes, who had gotten it from a *gentile* who had gotten it after he crossed the bay...it was impossible to determine for sure where the powder had originated, nor even that it was made from the bark of a tree. She had been told it would be good for treating the "swamp fever." But he remembered one of his professors in his medical training cautioning the students, "Don't argue with the diagnosis when the cure is effected." And the facts were clear to him: Father de Landaeta had all of the symptoms of malaria. A concoction specific to malaria brought him relief.

He couldn't wait to share this information with Father de Landaeta and when he did, the other priest smiled and observed, "Perhaps we are not the only ones who have something to teach in this meeting of cultures. I thought malaria was a disease of hot, humid climates."

"As did I," Father Juan answered, "but it is thought that it is spread through miasmas in the air. In fact, its name is, of course, Italian for 'bad air.' I have never seen such a place for miasmas as San Francisco." He gestured toward the fog rolling down the hillside. "Perhaps it is just because until now, we have never lived in an area with cold miasmas, that we have associated it with the tropics.

"When the unusual aspects of your sickness became obvious to me, I looked very carefully at the sickness of all of the Indians. Several of the spotted diseases are obviously prevalent, as they are in all of the missions. Interestingly, though, I found several instances of what have likely been the same as your illness, which I am now convinced is malaria. Malaria, I believe, is endemic to the marshy areas of California. Malaria may account for the difference in disease levels we have observed between San Francisco and the other missions, which of course are located in dryer, warmer areas."

"Malaria, you say," Father de Landaeta mused. He was intrigued by the unusual diagnosis.

"I would continue to drink Guadalupe's tea," Father Juan suggested. "If nothing else, think of the comfort you are bringing to some poor souls in purgatory." Both priests laughed, and Father Juan concluded, "I would like someday to visit with that Miwok shaman I have heard about on the other side of the bay, and talk with him about malaria. Of course, it won't be malaria in his language, but I think we have a reservoir of a unique disease in this bay."

"Let me know," the newly-affable Father de Landaeta said, "and I will have some of the neophytes take you over." As he left the superior's office, Father Juan had a feeling that perhaps, finally, he was making some headway.

Later that day, he was contemplating this interesting prospect and writing in his journal when a shadow blocked the light from his open door. He looked up to see Estella standing in the doorway. He had not listed her on one of his messages to Father de Landaeta, and so he was surprised to see her. He rose to greet her.

"Come in, come in Estella. Please have a seat. What can I do for you?"

Estella, once again garbed in the drab uniform of the neophytes, took a seat and declared, in a very matter of fact tone, "Tiburcio is telling people that you have asked him questions about what happened on the expedition."

Father Juan muttered a quiet imprecation. He could not remember if he had asked of Tiburcio the same vow of silence he had extracted from Xavier. *Probably it wouldn't have mattered*, he thought; the man had not impressed him as a very discrete person.

"Who is he telling this to?" he asked.

"Everyone in the village." She paused. "Probably everyone he sees. He is telling everyone that Father Juan is very interested in the 'great battle' that took place that day. Xavier and I have both asked him not to talk about this. I told you once, Father, that there was nothing the Spanish do that the Indians do not know about. It is also true that there is nothing the Indians say that the Spanish do not soon hear."

Father Juan was surprised to find himself asking her, "What should I do?"

The question was as startling to her as it had been to him. She looked at him curiously. "There is nothing you can do, Father. As soon as he told one person it was on its way to Father de Landaeta. I tell you this just so you will not be caught by surprise when you are questioned about it." She rose to leave. "*Buenas noches, Padre.*"

Father Juan sat back down at his desk and considered his next move. Estella's words came back to him: *There is nothing you can do, Father.* He decided to just wait and see.

He didn't have to wait long and see. As the monks were leaving the chapel after Lauds the next morning, Father de Landaeta beckoned to him.

"Juan, if you would please, visit with me in my study."

As the two priests sat down in the narrow room and availed themselves of the inevitable cup of hot chocolate, Father Juan noted that the superior was again looking very worn and drawn this morning.

"Are you well, Father?" he asked. "Has your fever returned?"

"I am fine, Juan," the priest replied with a wan smile. "I do not need some of Guadalupe's tea." He continued. "I have told you that one of my duties I find most burdensome is that of handling relations between the members of our orders. If I am distressed this morning, it is over such a matter." He took a long sip of his chocolate and continued thoughtfully.

"One of my friars feels that another of my friars is encouraging calumnies about him. He wants such talk stopped immediately, and he wants an apology."

Father Juan started to protest, and the superior held up a silencing hand. "Let me finish, Juan, and then you can answer." He let his hand fall, as if he could not summon strength even for the gesture. "Let us not play with words. Father Danti feels that you are encouraging the Indians in unfounded talk, that something terrible took place on his expedition last spring. He wants you admonished, and he wants all such talk stopped." The older priest paused. "Several months ago, I would have acceded without hesitation to his request. In the past several weeks, though, I think I have learned much. First, I have learned that you are a sincere and conscientious priest, and I might add, apparently a physician of some skill as well. More importantly, I have learned that Father Danti is an intemperate man. When I was assigned to this position, I was very unsure of my suitability for it. I dislike giving people orders and I dislike punishing people. Father Danti came shortly after I did. As I am sure you have noticed, he is a man who thrives on giving orders, and who does not hesitate to punish. I considered him the answer to my prayers. I would let him handle the temporal affairs of the mission and I would handle the spiritual. He relieved me of all of the duties I was ill-suited for. I happily turned my back on those duties. I was happy, and he was happy.

"But as time went on, I found to my dismay that while it is very easy to give people power, it is impossible to take it back. As one of his peripheral duties, Father Danti is the chaplain to the *presidio*. He enjoys the company of the soldiers. He spends a lot of his off-duty time with them. He likes the discipline of the military and the order it can bring. He believes that same sort of discipline can make our efforts with the Indians more successful. For the past couple of years, all of the Indians, neophyte and gentile, along with all of the soldiers from the *presidio*, began to see Father Danti as the head of Mission San Francisco. This did not bother me at all. As I said, I am ill-suited to a position of authority. San Francisco is the first and only mission I have ever been at. I thought our problem with runaways was simply something all of the missions suffered. I was surprised when you told me that the problem was far worse at San Francisco then at any of the other missions. Ever since you have arrived, I have been examining more carefully life here at Mission San Francisco, and...I do not like what I have seen. I consider myself to blame for that." He paused and continued purposefully. "I will be sending by the next messenger a request for my retirement to the College of San Fernando in Mexico City."

Pausing again, he sighed. "I am not suited for this life."

Once again, Father Juan started to protest, and once again, Father de

Landaeta held up a quieting hand. "These matters, as you probably know, do not move very quickly, so I am sure I will be here long enough for you to complete your investigations. I have learned, Juan, that you are a thorough and conscientious investigator. If your investigation has led you in a direction different than the one taken by other persons, I am confident it is because facts, not hearsay, have led you there. I am also confident that should the facts lead you to a conclusion other than the one you expected, you will not hesitate to embrace it and admit errors you have made. I do not feel that confidence with other members of my staff. Therefore, I encourage you to continue your investigation, and I will put no obstacles in your way." The superior leaned back in his chair with a decided air of satisfaction and finished, "Now, Father, you wanted to say something."

Father Juan did not know what to say. He had come to the meeting expecting to be chastised and to have his efforts frustrated. Instead, he had been encouraged to pursue his investigation with vigor.

"All I can say, Father, is thank you. If retirement to San Fernando College is what you want, I will pray that you get it. I would ask you to not be too harsh with yourself. Your decisions regarding the running of the mission were made with the best of intentions on your part. None of us can ever see into the future, and of course, to err is human. I promise you I will not misplace your confidence."

"I am sure you will not," the superior answered. "Let me stress, Father, what I have said. I will not place any obstacles in your way. I have not said you will not find any obstacles. As I understand it, you are planning on questioning some members of the military. You need to know that Father Danti has a very close relationship with the soldiers—perhaps too close. God bless your efforts."

Father Juan woke the next morning as he did every morning to the pealing of the bells calling the priests and the neophytes to Lauds. He splashed some water on his face, pulled on his robe, and walked out toward the chapel. He was surprised to be greeted by a clear, star-strewn sky. What he had taken to be a normal feature of San Francisco—the damp gray fog—was nowhere in evidence. And after morning prayer and Mass, he stepped out to a startlingly blue sky, again with not the slightest hint of any clouds or fog. The bay at the foot of the hills was as blue as the sky, and a very slight breeze broke its surface into a plate of sparkles. It was an invigorating, challenging day. He had to get out in it. Enough of reports and ponderings. Today would be a perfect day to take a walk to the *presidio* and begin talking to the soldiers.

He began walking. The mission was on one of the hills that were the defining feature of San Francisco Bay. The *presidio* was on the same hill, just slightly lower. In the bay, he could see the low-lying Yerba Buena, tiny Alcatraz and larger *Isla Angeles*.

He arrived at the *presidio* and sought out the colonel's office. Lieutenant Colonel Pedro de Alberni received him graciously.

"Good morning, Father, please come in." He barked an order to a young aide who disappeared and quickly returned with steaming cups of chocolate for the colonel and his guest. The colonel's office looked out directly on several cannon emplacements that stared straight at the entrance to the bay. No ship could enter San Francisco Bay without passing in front of the colonel's eyes and, more significantly, in front of those menacing-looking pieces of artillery. Colonel Alberni proudly pointed out the features of the fort below them.

"That is Fort *San Joaquin*. It has ten cannons, covering every aspect of the entrance to our bay." He smiled broadly and added, "There are two more cannon aimed back at the hills, should the Franciscans decide to invade us." Both men laughed at the joke and sat down to discuss the purpose of the monk's visit. He began with an explanation of his overall duties.

"I have been asked by the governor and by the father president of the Franciscans in California to examine the high rates of mortality and the high incidence of escapism Mission San Francisco is plagued with. I would like to visit with Corporal Montoya and perhaps privates..." here he consulted his notes ". . . Melendez, Galindo and Lopez." At the colonel's questioning look, he explained. "It has to do with an expedition they went on with Father Danti last year. The purpose of that expedition was to recover some fugitives from San Francisco. Unfortunately, not only were the fugitives not recovered, but there was a death of one of the members of their party. The circumstances of that death are what I am particularly interested in."

The colonel was immediately alert. "I remember that incident, Father. Corporal Montoya was clear in his report, and *I* want it to be clear that the army was no part of an effort to return fugitives. The army was simply there to protect the *padre*, and they fired only when a group of hostile natives first fired on them."

"I understand that, Colonel; that has been made very clear to me. The death of the man in question—his name was Francisco—apparently occurred very suddenly, almost without warning. It is that about which I am trying to get more information. If there is a disease lurking which can cause that sort of fulminant death, I want to know all I can about it."

The colonel considered this carefully and replied. "That was in the corporal's report. A neophyte got sick and died, and they buried him there near the mouth of the *San Joaquin* River." He shook his head slowly. "You know, Father, the official policy of the governor, and therefore of the army, is that we will not be part of efforts to forcefully return runaways from any of the missions. I approved that expedition last year only because I was assured by Father Danti that no force was intended. He was going to reason with the runaways and ask them to return. He wanted a military escort only because he was going into unfamiliar territory east of San Francisco." Again, he shook his head slowly. "We know how well that worked out: It became an armed confrontation with a large band of Indians. The corporal reports that his men did not comport themselves well. No runaways were returned. On top of that, we have the death of one of the expedition members from some unknown disease." He smiled ruefully. "No, that was not one of our more successful ventures, and I don't mind telling you I am still answering questions from Monterey about it." He rose. "I will get Sergeant Amador to get the men you wish to speak with. I will have them report to my office."

"I don't want to interfere with your day, Colonel. I wonder if I might just go about the *presidio* and talk to them as I find them. I might want to talk with other of the soldiers who were on that expedition. It is just these four whose names I have now."

The colonel smiled benignly and shook his head. "That is not the army way, Father. I am the colonel of this entire regiment. I can tell the regiment as a whole to march forward into deadly fire and they will obey. But I cannot tell one single man to do anything. I must tell the lieutenant, who will tell the sergeant, who will tell the corporal, who will tell the man." He smiled again, "*That* is the army way. We will find a small office for you and send the men there to talk with you. Sergeant!" he shouted towards an office down the hall.

Very shortly, Father Juan stood in the doorway of a small storage room, which some soldiers had cleared by piling everything along one back wall. He had given the sergeant the names of Corporal Montoya as well as Privates Galindo, Melendez and Lopez. Melendez, it turned out, had been promoted to corporal since the expedition and transferred to the *presidio* in Monterey. He would not be available to be interviewed. Sergeant Amador reassured him that the names of all of the soldiers on that expedition would be recorded and he would make them available to the priest.

The sergeant left to summon the soldiers. Father Juan awaited his first visitor and watched the activity of the fort. A tall figure loomed in his doorway. *"Buenas dias, Padre.* You wanted to see me?" The two chevrons on his jacket sleeve told Father Juan that it was Corporal Montoya who stood before him.

"Good afternoon, Corporal. Please, come in, have a seat." He turned from the door and gestured to him to come in. As the corporal took the indicated chair, Father Juan explained his mission and his objectives. The soldier sat, occasionally nodding, never taking his eyes from the priest, and offering no comments of his own.

"So," Father Juan concluded with false enthusiasm, "I would like you to talk to me about the expedition last winter to recover some runaways."

"That was a long time ago, Father." the corporal offered.

"Well yes," urged the priest, "but you must remember much of it. The colonel has given me a copy of the report you filed." Here he slightly lifted from his desk a piece of paper.

"If the colonel has given you a copy of my report, what more do you need from me?"

Father Juan could see that this man was not going to be one of his more forthcoming witnesses. "Corporal," he said, picking up the report and scanning it quickly, "I am not much interested in the tactical or military aspects of that expedition. It is of little consequence to me how many leagues you marched on day one or day two, what direction you went in, or why you picked a particular site as opposed to another to camp for the night."

"Then what can I tell you, *Padre*?" the truculent corporal asked.

Sighing, and letting the report fall back on the desk Father Juan began again. "Corporal, I am trying to determine the circumstances of the only death that occurred on that expedition."

"An *Indio,*" the corporal interrupted him.

"Yes, an *Indio* named Francisco," Father Juan agreed.

"Then you should be talking to your brother Franciscan, Father Danti, not me. I am a soldier of the Spanish army. I was on that expedition to provide safety to Father Danti. I was not on that mission to worry about any of his neophytes, and believe me, I did not."

"Corporal," Father Juan said with resignation, "I have talked with Father Danti. I plan to talk further with Father Danti, but until I do let me just ask you: How did Francisco die?"

The corporal shrugged, "He got sick and he died. You are the physician, Father. I am, as I said, simply a soldier."

Father Juan decided to try a different approach. "Did you help bury him?" he asked abruptly.

Here the corporal shifted uncomfortably. "Well, yes, I and the other soldiers helped Father Danti bury him."

"You and the other soldiers?"

"Yes."

"Why?" the priest asked.

"Why?" the incredulous soldier answered. "Why? Because he was dead! Is it not one of the works of mercy to bury the dead? Why, indeed!" he sputtered.

"Excuse me, Corporal," a soothing Father Juan offered. "I have not been clear. What I meant was, why did the *soldiers* have to bury an Indian who had died? There were several Indians in the party. Would it not have made sense to have the Indians perform that chore, rather than members of the king's army?"

A now decidedly guarded Corporal Montoya sat back in his chair and glared at the priest. "The *Indios* were not with us at the time. They were ahead of us looking for the runaways. Father Danti said that because we did not know what disease the man had died of, we should bury him as quickly as possible to avoid spreading the disease."

Father Juan picked up the corporal's report and read through it again. "This would have been on the third of March, the second day of the expedition, is that correct?"

"If that is what it says in my report, that is when it was," the corporal growled.

"Tell me, Corporal, do you remember what the symptoms of this man's sickness were?"

"I do not. I pay no attention to the *Indios*. They are not my responsibility. Whether converted or not, the *Indios* are the complete responsibility of the Franciscans. That has been made very clear to us. If one of my men had been sick, I would have known of it. I don't care if an *Indio* is sick." He felt compelled to add with a defiant smile, "I don't care if an *Indio* dies."

"Thank you, Corporal, you have been helpful." As the corporal rose to leave the priest asked him one more question. "Corporal, do you remember where it was that Francisco was buried?"

The soldier stopped and gave a dismissive grunt and an expansive wave of this hand. "In the *pantanos*, Father." He turned and left.

¤ 13

The interviews continued until early afternoon. Private Lopez had virtually nothing to offer. The private, Father Juan noted, was not Spanish nor Mexican, but one of the local natives. When asked, he told Father Juan that he was Patwin, "from further north." The soldiers had appeared at his village some time ago and recruited young men for the army. He had been offered money, food and a life of ease in the army. Father Juan did not bother to ask him if the promises had been fulfilled.

"But your name is Mexican," Father Juan noted.

The private gave a blank stare and replied, "That is the name they gave me when I joined the army. They said they could not write or pronounce the name my people had given me, so they told me, 'You will be Lopez, your name in the army is Lopez,' and that is what they wrote down." He shrugged "I am Private Lopez."

Private Lopez was dressed in a worn, ill-fitting uniform that had obviously been handed down to him. Probably, Father Juan guessed, from some other, since-deceased "Private Lopez." The haircuts of all of the soldiers generally left any sense of style far behind, but in Private Lopez's case, it was a particularly distressing thatch of black hair that looked as if it had been attacked with a bayonet. The private sat in the tiny office visibly shaking and nervous, and nothing Father Juan said or did could make him more at ease. He was practically incoherent in his responses, which consisted almost totally of "*Si, Padre*," or "*No, Padre*," usually blurted out before the priest had even finished his question.

"Did you help bury—" "*No, Padre!*" "—the Indian Francisco? Did you see his body—" "*No, Padre!*" "—before it was buried? Were you there when he died?"

"I don't know, *Padre*; I don't know when he died."

"Did you fire your musket—"

"*Si, Padre*, we all fired our muskets!"

Father Ibarra gave him an exasperated look. "Let me finish, son. Did you fire your musket at the fleeing Indians?"

"I fired my musket, *Padre*, when everyone else fired their muskets. I am not sure what we were firing at; some *Indios* were firing arrows at us."

"How many times did you fire?"

"I don't know, *Padre*; I know we reloaded at least once. Maybe more times, maybe not. I do not know, *Padre*."

Father Juan decided that the terrified young soldier had nothing to add to the facts he already had, thanked him, and dismissed him.

Private Galindo, when he appeared, was an entirely different story. He was clearly Spanish or *crijole*. He carried himself confidently, and wore a uniform that was clean and well-fitting. He told Father Juan that he had been in army for three years, and he found it to his liking. He had joined from a small village in Sonora, and after a brief posting in northern Mexico, had been sent to Alta California. He liked California and the army, and he hoped to make corporal and maybe someday sergeant.

He remembered very well the expedition of last March. He was the scout for his squad. He had the best sense of place and direction of all of the soldiers, and he was often used when they were going into new territory. He knew how to read and write, rare accomplishments among the common soldiers. He had been taught by the army how to draw maps, and had been mapmaker on the expedition in question. Father Juan made a careful note of this last. He asked the young man if he had made maps of the entire expedition.

"Oh yes, Father, I drew where we camped, where we started from each day, where we had the battle with the runaways."

"Did you draw where the Indian Francisco was buried?"

"Yes, Father, that is on one of my maps."

"Where are your drawings?"

The young man shrugged. "Each day I give them to the corporal. He gives them to the sergeant, the sergeant I suppose gives them to the lieutenant, the lieutenant I suppose gives them to the colonel."

Father Juan thought again of the mind-numbing bureaucracy of the military and its obsession with the "chain of command." He pawed quickly through the reports the colonel had given him. There were no drawings included. He began asking the soldier the same questions he had asked of the others: Had Francisco seemed sick, what were his symptoms, how had he died? The answers were the same.

"I do not pay much attention to the *Indios*, Father," he smiled apologetically. "They have their own ways and they do not like to be around soldiers, they stay apart. I do not remember anyone being sick on that march, but...?"

"Tell me about the day you ran into the runaways."

"Oh, that day." He rolled his eyes. "You know, Father, I have been in the army for three years and that is the first time I have ever fired my musket except during a drill. I will remember that day forever. It was the second day. The corporal had told the neophytes to spread out and go ahead of us. He told them to walk quietly, and to watch for signs of the runaways."

"All of the neophytes?" the priest asked. At the young man's questioning look he explained. "I mean, were all of the neophytes sent out ahead of the soldiers?"

"No," Private Galindo answered thoughtfully. "Francisco was kept behind. Perhaps because he was sick?" he added brightly.

"Perhaps," the priest replied non-committedly. "Please continue with your story."

"Well, we had been marching for several hours." He paused and elaborated. "Marching is not the right word. There is no way to march in the *pantanos*. You just slog along as best you can. We were spread out all over the place. The corporal had to keep telling us, 'Close up, close up,' and then," here he smiled, "'Spread out, spread out, don't bunch up!' In the early afternoon, one of the Indians who had been sent ahead came running back. 'We've found them,' he said, 'they're up ahead, we've found them.' Now everything got very confused, everyone started shouting. Father Danti started running forward, we *all* started running forward, the corporal was shouting, Father Danti was shouting. When we came in sight of the *Indio* runaways, they stopped and started shooting arrows at us. Everyone was shouting, and suddenly some of the soldiers began firing at the runaways. I stopped and fired my musket, but we could see the runaways disappearing into the brush. I stopped to reload my musket, when all of a sudden, the corporal was shouting 'Cease fire, cease fire!' while Father Danti was shouting, 'Catch them, catch them!' The neophytes were screaming, and the runaways were scattering. As I was reloading again, one more shot was fired, then all the shooting stopped. The corporal was still calling to us to cease fire, and Father Danti was still shouting, calling the neophytes names. I had reloaded but did not fire again because of the corporal's order.

"I looked around, unsure of what we should do next. Behind me, I saw the corporal grab hold roughly of Father Danti. They both looked back in the direction we had just come from. The corporal was saying something to Father Danti and pointing backward. Finally, the corporal shouted to the neophytes, 'Stand fast, stay where you are, stand fast.' He and Father Danti started to walk back. Just then, one of the neophytes who had been hiding in the grass stood up and began walking back towards us. 'Stay where you are,' the corporal shouted, while Father Dante called to the neophyte, 'Go after them!' But this neophyte kept walking back toward us. The corporal grabbed the musket from one of the soldiers—I think it was Lopez—and fired near the neophyte. 'Stay where you are,' he shouted. And still Father Danti kept screaming, 'Go after them, go after them!' The neophyte turned, and he and all of the other neophytes began walking away, in the direction the *Indios* had gone.

"I and the other soldiers stood there and looked at the corporal. 'Stay where you are,' he commanded. He handed the musket back to Lopez, and he and the father began again to retrace our steps to where we'd been when the messenger arrived. They walked perhaps half a league, and stopped. They were discussing something; I could not tell what. The corporal was shaking his head and Father Danti just stood there, staring at the ground. After some time, I don't remember how long, the corporal motioned for us to come back. The corporal and Father Danti were standing next to a body, wrapped in a blanket. They told us it was the neophyte, Francisco. They said he had been sick and that he had died just before the attack began. We dug a grave and buried him right there. Then the corporal told me to run forward and bring the neophytes back. He said that we would march back to the mission, and that we would camp for the night near where we had camped before. He told me to bring the neophytes back and that we were going to return to the mission."

"What did you do then?" Father Juan asked. The young soldier looked nonplussed.

"I ran forward to find the neophytes. It was easy to track them because of the crushed reeds. I finally found them about two leagues away, and told them we were all returning to the mission." Here he paused for a minute. "They spoke among themselves for a bit. I do not know what they were saying, but I got the idea that some of them did not want to go back."

You came very close to dying right there, my friend, thought Father Juan.

The private finished, "Finally, they agreed to go back, and we started back."

The priest interrupted him. "Did you and this group go past Francisco's grave on the trip back?"

"We went near it, but not past it, and I felt it was best not to tell the Indians that one of their brothers was buried there. We caught up with the others just as it was getting dark and they were setting up camp for the night. We camped there, and the next morning we started back for the mission."

"Was anything said about Francisco's death?"

"One of the neophytes asked where Francisco was, and Father Danti told him that he had died and had been buried."

"Nothing else was said?"

"No...except..." He paused.

"Except what?" the priest insisted.

"That night, we were talking among ourselves. As soldiers do. We were laughing at some of the foolish things we had done that afternoon, and about how much confusion there had been. Corporal Montoya suddenly stood up and said angrily 'There is nothing to be laughing about. That was the worst case of fire discipline I have ever seen. Who gave the order to fire?' When no one answered his question, he answered it himself. 'No one!' he shouted. 'No one gave the order to fire. Someone just decided to shoot at a bunch of *Indios* in the woods and you all started firing. You were the poorest excuse I've ever seen for Spanish soldiers. When we get back to the *presidio,* you can tell all of your girlfriends in town to just forget about you, because I am going to have you drilling twenty-four hours a day for the next month. It was a disgrace!'"

"Anything else?" the priest asked.

The young soldier hung his head sheepishly. "He told us, 'If you know what is good for you, will not talk about this with anyone. We are lucky someone wasn't killed.'"

"When you were firing, Private, were any of the runaways hit?"

The young soldier smiled sheepishly again. "I don't know, Father; I was just firing. I don't think I ever really aimed at anything, I just fired because everyone else was firing."

"Thank you, Private, this has been helpful. You may go."

He sat back and considered the growing pile of notes he had taken. He knew he would have to do some careful sifting of facts, but he knew also that there was useful information in the stories he had heard. He decided to head back to the mission. Before he did, he stopped in the colonel's office to thank him for his help. The colonel was out, "gone down to the waterfront to greet a newly-arrived ship," as the sergeant informed him.

"Well, please thank the colonel for me for his cooperation; and thank you, Sergeant, for arranging the interviews."

"Anytime," the sergeant answered. "If there is anything else we can do, please let me know."

He suddenly remembered Private Galindo's recitation. "Perhaps there is something, Sergeant. I understand there may have been some maps or drawings made of the route of that expedition. Would it be possible for me to see those? They were not included with the copies of the corporal's report I received."

"I will check with the colonel, Father. I do remember some maps in that report. We will arrange to send them to you."

"One other thing, Sergeant, if you would. Could you tell me what sort of man Corporal Montoya is?"

"Montoya is a good corporal. When his time comes, he will be made a sergeant, I am sure. He cares very much for his men. He drives them hard, and expects a lot from them, but in return he will always stand up for them. He will do all he can do to protect them. Not all corporals will do that. He felt that their performance on that expedition was not up to his standards, and he drilled them mercilessly after that. He does that, though, for their own good, to protect them. He is a good corporal," he repeated.

After thanking the sergeant again, Father Juan walked slowly back from the *presidio* to the mission. The day remained sunny and clear; the late afternoon might even have been characterized as warm.

¤ 14

Father Juan had organized all his notes and constructed what he felt was a detailed chronology of the recent illnesses of the Indians, and a detailed chronology of the events of last year.

A few days after his visit to the *presidio*, a young soldier appeared with a pouch for Father Juan. It was the promised maps, perhaps more accurately described as detailed drawings, of the expedition's travels. There were four of them. The first, labeled "Day One," showed the northern end of the bay and the alluvial plain of the *"Rio San Joaquin."* The second, "Encampment: Day One," was a fairly detailed plan showing *"Padre's* tent," "corporal's tent," "soldiers' tents," and *"Indio's* pallets," around a circle labeled "central fire." Also shown on this drawing were two small squares some distance from the encampment, labeled "Guard Post 1" and "Guard Post 2." Father Juan knew little about the proper disposition of sleeping troops, so he found little of interest in this drawing. It was the third drawing which captured his attention.

This drawing was labeled "Engagement with the *Indios."* He bemusedly noted that the title, with careful military deflection, failed to answer the question of whether or not a battle had been fought. He found himself admiring the dissimilitude of the military.

This drawing had some very definite features to it. Along the left edge ran a broad, curving double line, lightly shaded in and labeled, *"Rio San Joaquin."* Along the right edge was a densely-plotted series of what were meant to be trees, with notations at various points: *"Indios* here." It was the center of the drawing, though, that drew the priest's interest. It showed a line of stick men, some individually labeled: "Cpl. Mont.", "Fr. Dan.", "Pvt. Lopez", "Private Mel." Further forward was a small circle with an "x" in it, and forward of this, groups of stick men denoted *"neophitos."* The neophytes were closest to the woods, the soldiers and priest slightly further back towards the river. Most intriguing of all was a small cross, behind all of the people represented in the scene. It was labeled, "RIP Franc." There was an arrow labeled "N" on the lowest right-hand corner of the map, and the private's signature. There were straight lines drawn from various points to various points, always at least two, and sometimes three of the lines crossing. Father Juan knew enough about maps and navigation to realize they were lines of azimuth, and looking carefully he saw the notations 045°, 273°, 068°, etc. Three of the lines intersected at the "RIP" notation. There was a very rough scale indicating that from the river to the woods where the runaways had disappeared was about three leagues. The fourth drawing was labeled "Encampment: Day Two" and was the same detailed showing of how the party had been disposed for the night.

Father Juan studied the third drawing until he had it memorized. In fact, because he knew he would have to return it to the *presidio*, he made a copy for himself, tracing it on a translucent piece of paper. He decided that he would return the drawings to the *presidio* the very next day. He would return the drawings *and* have another talk with Private Galindo.

After breakfast the next morning, he took the originals and his own drawings and returned to the *presidio*. He went first to the sergeant's office, where he returned the maps and thanked the sergeant for the use of them. Preparing to leave he asked the sergeant, "Would you mind, Sergeant, if I spoke with Private Galindo again before I leave?"

The sergeant reminded him of the "chain of command." "You must ask Corporal Montoya if you can speak with Private Galindo. I do not know what plans the corporal may have for the private this morning."

"Of course, of course, Sergeant. Would it be all right if I ask Corporal Montoya if I may speak with Private Galindo?"

The sergeant gave a broad smile. Perhaps the *padre* was finally getting the concept. "By all means, Father. I think you will find Corporal Montoya with his soldiers out behind the corrals. They were going to select some new horses from a bunch that just came in. *Buenas dias, Padre.*"

Father Juan left the sergeant's office and set out in search of the corporal, wondering how the army ever got anything done in anything approaching an expeditious fashion. He had to admit, though, that the Franciscan bureaucracy was just as structured and rigid. No priest would ever think of approaching the father president without first talking with his immediate superior.

He found the corporal sitting on the top rail of a corral watching several of the soldiers wrestle with a herd of snorting, bucking horses. The corporal was laughing and shouting words of encouragement to the young men who seemed decidedly intimidated by the animals. Father Juan draped his arms over the rail and stood watching. The corporal glanced quickly down at him and then gave his attention back to the center of the corral.

"You are the boss," he shouted, "show him you are the boss, but show him you are a gentle boss, a kind boss."

"Like you, Corporal?" one of the young soldiers asked, with a grin.

"Yes, yes, just like me, you impudent pup!" the broadly smiling corporal shouted back.

The soldier finally got a halter over the horse's neck, and with a series of pats, strokes and soft words, got the horse to calm down and even follow him as he walked slowly around the corral. Father Juan noticed that it was Private Galindo leading the horse.

"He has a way with horses," he offered.

Without taking his gaze from the scene in front of him, the corporal responded, "He does, he does indeed. He is a good soldier and will be a fine horseman." He added musingly, "No matter how long he is in the army and no matter where he goes, he will always remember this, his first horse, that he trained at San Francisco." Breaking his reverie, he leaped down from the rail, brushed the seat of his trousers and turned to Father Juan.

"What can I do for you, *Padre*?" he asked.

"Actually, Corporal, I am here to seek your permission to visit once again with Private Galindo."

The corporal glanced quickly at the young soldier, and then fixed the *padre* with a studied stare. "Yes," he said abruptly, "I will get him for you." He walked off to the center of the corral, took the halter from Private Galindo, and pointed back to the priest standing at the rail. The private walked over to Father Juan. He bent to scramble through the rails of the corral and stood before the priest.

"Yes, Father, what can I do for you?"

Father Juan led him over to a small open shed with several benches in it. He sat on one of the benches and motioned for the young soldier to do the same. He took from the pouch his copies of the private's drawing, and asked him, "Do you recognize this, Private?"

"Of course; it is my drawing of the battle with the *Indios* last March." He corrected himself. "It is a *drawing* of my drawing of the battle with the *Indios*."

"That is correct, Private, I drew it from a tracing of your drawing. Have I been accurate in copying it?"

The soldier studied the drawing, turning his head slightly and then the drawing, before agreeing. "You have not put the mountains to the west that I had behind the forest. Nor the bearing lines I had drawn."

"I am sorry, Private. I was interested in the details of the battle, and I thought the mountains were just put in as sort of a border. They are far away from the battle site, are they not?"

"Yes," the soldier answered. "They are so far away that they had nothing to do with the battle, but" he added, "should we ever want to return to that place, the positions of the mountains, of one peak to the other, as well as the curves of the river," here he poked a finger at his sketch of the river, "that I used to plot, positions us when we were there, at the exact spot."

"Ah," the priest sighed. "I see, so the mountains are landmarks."

"Yes," the soldier answered. "With my drawing, if I were in that area again, I could look at the mountains on my drawing and the mountains on the ground and the curves of the river, take some compass readings, and I would know if I was near the site of the battle."

"I see," the priest repeated, with a newfound respect for the young man's mapmaking skills.

"Other than that, though," the private continued, "Yes, I think it is a good copy. I would have to see again my drawing to be sure, but I think it is a good copy."

"Private, I would like to ask you some questions about this drawing. First, why did you draw it?"

"That is my job. The army requires a detailed report accompanied by illustrations of every significant action any troops are engaged in. The corporal does the reports—he used to do the drawings, too, but he says I have much more talent at that, so he had me do this one." He added modestly, "He says it was very good, better than he could have done, and he will have me do them all from now on."

"I noticed, Private, that you also did drawings of your two encampments. What is the purpose of those?"

The private smiled. "That is not an army requirement but a corporal requirement. Most usually a squad of soldiers in Alta California does not put out guards when it stops for the night. The natives are not usually a threat. Corporal Montoya says that he doesn't care what everybody else does, he always posts guards, and he wants drawings of them done so that he can use them to teach us how to properly guard ourselves in the wilderness. In the case of the expedition, the corporal had us camp so that the river protected us to the north and the west. So, he had sentries placed to the east and the south."

"Am I correct, Private, that you did this drawing—or rather your own drawing—and gave it to the corporal, who he filed it with his report, and you haven't seen it since?"

"No," the soldier replied thoughtfully, "We have all reviewed my drawing several times. The corporal has used them to teach us some lessons."

"Oh?" the priest asked. "What would be some of those lessons?"

"Well," the private began, pointing to the drawing, "see here where I have listed the soldiers and Father Danti and myself?"

"Excuse me, Private; I do not see your name except at the bottom of the map, although the others names are listed. Where are you?"

"This is me." He pointed to the circle with the *x* in it. "I would always be the circle with the *x*." He continued. "All of us soldiers and Father Danti are somewhat in a line from front to back. This is very bad according to the corporal. None of us has a clear 'field of fire' without endangering our comrades. We should be more out in line from side to side, instead of front to back. Also," he moved his finger to the right, "the *Indios* in the woods are about five hundred *varas* away. That is too far away. We never should have been firing at them from that distance. Our fire was very ineffective."

"If I remember, Private, you don't know for sure if any of them were hit."

"I do not, Father. The corporal says he doubts that any were." He looked carefully at the map. "From here," and he put his finger on the river, "to here," moving his finger to the circle with the *x* "is about two and a half leagues."

Leaving that finger in place he put another finger on the notation for the runaways, in the woods. "This is about five hundred *varas*, and the neophytes" he traced his finger forward, "were probably two or three hundred *varas* from both us and the runaways."

"And this?" Father Juan asked, pointing to the RIP notation. "I take it that this is Francisco's grave? How far behind *you*," he pointed to the private's location on the map, "is this?"

"Perhaps one hundred fifty or two hundred *varas*." As the private gave each of his guesses on distance the priest noted them on his copy of the map.

"Thank you, Private; you have been very helpful. Thank you; and—" the priest looked up at the corral, "good luck with your horse."

"Thank you, *Padre, buenas dias*." The young soldier trotted back to the corral and, exchanging a few brief words with the corporal, took his horse back. Father Juan sat in the shade of the shed for a few minutes and continued his notes. Rising to return to the mission, he passed the corporal who gave him a semi-salute and a neutral, *"Buenas dias, Padre."*

When he got back to the mission and settled himself in his office, he reviewed all that he had learned in the past several weeks. Only one narrative was missing: that of Father Danti. Other than their brief and unpleasant discussion of the incident several weeks ago, he and Father Danti had spoken no more about it. He realized that if he was going to prepare a report to the governor, and particularly if he was going to pursue his investigation beyond this point, he would have to give Father Danti a final opportunity to give his account. He first sought out Father de Landaeta and told him of his plan.

"I am going to ask Father Danti to sit down with me and give me his version of the events of last March," he told the superior.

Father de Landaeta smiled grimly and told him, "That will not be a pleasant conversation, Father, nor," he hesitated briefly, "am I sure it will be a very fruitful one."

"I realize that," Father Juan replied. "It is because it may become unpleasant that I feel compelled to be sure you know of it in advance. I am sure you will hear of it after the fact."

"As I told you earlier, Juan, I will put no obstacle in your way. You realize, of course, Father Danti is under no compulsion to talk with you."

"I know that. I will make it clear, though, that I am preparing to send a report to the governor and the father president, and that report will go, with or without his version. I think he will probably decide to talk with me."

"Tell me, Father Juan, what is it that you are looking for? You have been told by both Father Danti and by the corporal that Francisco died of a sudden sickness. Although it has been suggested to you by other people that they do not believe Francisco died of an illness, they have not suggested any other way in which he may have died. What is it you think that you might discover about his death?"

"I am not looking for anything in particular. I think it is likely that the accounts we have received of Francisco's death are probably accurate. As you know, Estella has her doubts, and I have heard enough from all sources, including Father Danti, that he certainly died very suddenly. If in fact it was a disease that killed Francisco, it was certainly a fulminating process of the worst sort. I think it is my duty to find out as much as I can about that process. I have told Estella that I would try to answer her questions, and in particular that I would try to help her properly bury her husband's remains. None of us can argue with that desire. Interestingly, as a result of a recent conversation I have had with a very bright young soldier, we are probably in a very good position to locate his remains."

"I am not sure, Juan, you are going to get much support from the army for an expedition to recover the remains of an *Indio*. Good luck, Father," was the superior's somewhat doubtful closing comment.

Later that afternoon, Father Juan approached Father Danti. "Antonio, I wonder if I might take some of your time, and have you visit with me for a bit about the expedition to the San Joaquin last March.

"I will have no time this afternoon," the other priest replied. "Perhaps tomorrow."

"Tomorrow, after breakfast? Father Juan asked.

"Tomorrow, sometime," was the curt reply.

"My brother," Father Juan persisted, "we need to pick a time. Tomorrow; shall we say tomorrow right after siesta, three o'clock? Would that work?"

"Fine, tomorrow at three o'clock. I'll come to your office," Father Danti finally relented.

"*Bueno, bueno, gracias Antonio; hasta manana.*"

15

It was really no surprise to Father Juan when three o'clock the next afternoon came and went, and Father Danti was nowhere to be seen. He had come too far on this quest to just abandon it, however, because of one recalcitrant priest. He walked out into the courtyard of the mission and asked a passing neophyte if he knew where Father Danti was.

"He went to the *presidio* this morning, Father; he was expected back by now."

The fact that Father Danti, when faced with the inevitability of providing some detail about his ill-fated expedition last spring, would check with the soldiers at the *presidio*, was not surprising. All Father Juan could do now was wait. His fellow priest did not keep him waiting too long. It was just before four o'clock when Father Danti appeared in his doorway.

"Good afternoon, Father, I am sorry I am a little late. I had some business to conduct at the *presidio*. I am the chaplain there, you know."

"Yes, I know, and I understand, Father. Thank you for finding the time to visit with me." As the other priest settled himself, Father Juan offered him some water and began."As you know, Antonio, my primary mission here is to look into the death rate of the neophytes, which, I think you also know, is inordinately high."

The other friar simply nodded, and Father Juan continued. "I don't know how much Father de Landaeta has told you about my investigation, but I have uncovered evidence, I think, of a new disease in San Francisco."

"Really?" Father Danti asked with genuine surprise.

"Yes, I believe that in addition to the diseases which are common to most of the neophyte population, San Francisco harbors in its damp airs the causative miasma of malaria. My research is far from complete, but I think when all of the evidence in, we will unfortunately be able to add malaria to one of the ills that plagues this mission."

"That is very interesting," Father Danti added, now with real interest. "Perhaps that is the disease that killed that *Indio* you were so concerned about."

"His name was Francisco," Father Juan reminded his visitor, "and you are right, his death has been a puzzle to me. You see, nothing I have heard from the others on the expedition suggests malaria as the disease that killed

Francisco. Actually, malaria seldom kills healthy adults. It affects them for years afterward, but it is seldom fatal in its acute stage."

Now Father Danti showed a clear irritation. "Well, then, what the h—... what do you think killed him?"

"I don't know, Antonio, and I thought you might help me. As I understand it, he went from being healthy and alert to dead in less than twenty-four hours. That is an extremely virulent course, and I am afraid that malaria may not be the only unexpected disease at Mission Dolores." His use of the nickname was deliberate. "If you would, Antonio, please give me your remembrances of how Francisco was on that expedition."

"I've already told you. I don't spend my time responding to every complaint of an ache or pain from the *Indios*."

Father Juan pressed the attack. "This was not an ache or pain, Antonio. This was death. I cannot believe that a young man just suddenly fell over dead with no complaint."

Father Danti replied almost dismissively. "I suppose he said something that morning, 'Father, I don't feel well,' or 'Father, I am sick.' Yes, now that I recall it, he did say something to that effect."

"When was that?" Father Juan asked.

"I don't know, that morning, just after breakfast, just as we started out on our day's march."

"Was that why you kept him back with your party, instead of sending him off with the other neophytes?"

"Perhaps."

"You have already told me several times, Father, that you did not spend your time catering to the whims of ill or complaining Indians. Why then would you keep him back with you?"

Father Danti leaned back in his chair and now fixed the other priest with a cold stare.

"Do not put words into my mouth, Juan. I said 'perhaps,' and that was in response to your suggestion that might have been the reason why I kept him back. *Perhaps* I kept him back because his name simply came up." Noticing Father Juan's questioning look he added, "You have not spent any time with the military, I believe?" Adopting an air of superiority, he went on. "If you had, you would know that whenever a disposition of troops is split up, each contingent keeps aside a messenger. The day before, it would have been someone else, the next day another one. I simply chose Francisco as the messenger we would use to send information forward to the neophytes who were in advance of us. His illness, if such he was displaying, had nothing to do with it."

"When did Francisco die?" Father Juan asked.

"I am not really sure. Late that morning or early that afternoon. Just before we spotted the runaways."

"He—just as I said earlier—he just fell over dead?"

"Of course not!" the other exploded. "He had been whining and complaining ever since we left. 'Father, I feel ill, Father, I am hot, Father, I can't go on.' I realize now that I should have paid more attention to his complaints. But what if I had? I am no physician, I had no medicine, I had nothing to offer him. I could have told him to lie down and rest, but that would have just meant that when he died, he would be further away from us. Perhaps we never would have found him. Perhaps we never *should* have found him." He added bitterly, "Because I gave him a Christian burial, I am now being hounded mercilessly about this stupid neophyte. Because I gave him a Christian burial, you have interrogated the corporal and the soldiers..." Realizing he might have gone too far, he stopped abruptly. "What more do you wish to know?"

"Where were the others when he died?"

"The other neophytes were far ahead of us, the soldiers were a little ahead of us, and the corporal, Francisco and I were bringing up the rear."

"And then?" Father Juan let the open-ended question hang in the area.

Father Danti was in no mood to play into the other priest's hands. "And then what?" he asked defiantly.

Father Juan continued patiently. "You and Francisco were in the rear of the column. The soldiers were in front of you, and quite a bit further ahead were the neophytes. Francisco *may have* been complaining or he *may have* just been marching silently along. What happened next?"

"Everything," Father Danti snorted disdainfully. "One of the neophytes came running back, shouting, 'We've found them!' The soldiers started running ahead, the runaways started shooting arrows at us, the soldiers started shooting, the corporal started shouting, the runaways ran into the woods, and the stupid neophytes began hiding in the reeds. Everything happened, and nothing." He shook his head slowly. "Finally, we got the neophytes to quit hiding and go after the runaways. 'Go after them, go after them,' I ran towards them and urged them on. They trotted off half-heartedly."

"When did you discover that Francisco was dead?' Father Juan asked.

"After I had gotten the neophytes to follow the runaways, I walked back to the soldiers. Corporal Montoya was a little further back. '*Padre*,' he called. 'Come here.' I joined him perhaps twenty *varas* back. He was looking down at Francisco's body, which was lying on the ground."

"He was dead?" Father Juan asked.

"No," the other said sarcastically, "he was taking an early *siesta*. Yes, he was dead; I checked to see if I could hear his heart and the corporal held a metal signal mirror up to his mouth. He was dead."

"And then you buried him?"

"I wrapped him in his blanket. We were afraid of the disease that killed him leaving his body and killing us. The corporal called the soldiers back and they dug a shallow grave. I said some prayers and we buried him." Father Danti leaned back in his chair with a challenging stare. "That is what happened to Francisco, and anyone who tells you otherwise is lying."

"No one has told me otherwise," Father Juan answered him calmly. "I am sure you know the corporal has filed a report of the expedition, and his story is *exactly* the same as yours." He had unconsciously stressed the word "exactly."

"Well, then," Father Danti stood. "There you have it. Complete your report and send it off, and allow us to return to our duties."

"Thank you, *fray*," Father Juan answered. "I appreciate your help. I will indeed prepare my report and send it off."

When the other priest left, he stood and decided to take a walk around the mission. He went out the side gate, toward the cemetery, and then continued further west. *My work is finished.* He mulled the idea over in his head. He had interviewed all of the appropriate persons. He had gotten a story that was plausible, if questionable. He had nothing to suggest that the official version was not the true version. Yet, something gnawed at his mind. He couldn't help but think, *My work is finished, but it is not complete.* What was he missing? What was he failing to do? The obvious answer was that he would fail to bring closure to Estella's doubts. He would have to tell her that he had no reason to doubt that her husband had died of disease and that he was buried, somewhere in the *pantanos*. He knew that would be disappointing to her, but it was the only answer he could give.

As he walked back into the mission compound he came upon Xavier, leaving after his days' work.

"*Buenas tardes, Padre.*"

"*Buenas tardes, Xavier,*" the priest returned. "How was your day?"

The Indian smiled. "My day was fine, Father; and yours? How is your investigation going?"

"It is going fine; it is almost finished. I will soon send my report to the governor."

"Father?" the young man questioned, "I am very soon going to send my petition to Father de Landaeta that I may leave the mission and live in town. I am ready to live on my own and make a living as a stone mason." Here he lowered his voice somewhat, and continued in a conspiratorial tone, "There are already some businessmen in town who have seen my work, and who have asked me to do some projects for them."

"Why, that is wonderful, Xavier, just wonderful! I am very happy for you. I am sure your petition will be granted."

"Well," the Indian continued, "just to be sure, I wondered if I could ask you to write a letter of recommendation. A petition to the father superior is always better if there is a recommendation from one of the Franciscans with it."

"Of course, Xavier, I would be not only pleased, but honored to write such a recommendation. When do you need it?"

"Probably by the end of the week. I have not yet submitted my petition and I am planning to give it to Father de Landaeta on Saturday, at the end of the week."

"Just let me know, Xavier, when the father superior has your petition, and I will be sure he has my recommendation the very same day."

"Good, Father, good," was the smiling reply. "I will let you know." He turned to continue on and then stepped back. "Did you know, Father, that Tiburcio has left again?"

The monk gave a questioning look and replied, "I, uh, I'm not sure I know what you mean?"

"Tiburcio has run away from the mission. He left two nights ago." He smiled. "Tiburcio has run away before, last year sometime. In fact, that was one of the reasons he was picked for the expedition last year. Father Danti told him that he must know the way the runaways had gone, and he must lead us to them. If he didn't, he would be punished." He smiled slightly and continued, "He did lead us to the runaways on that expedition."

"Why did he run away now?"

Xavier paused just slightly and then answered. "Tiburcio told us that Father Danti had punished him for talking to you, and for 'spreading lies.' Tiburcio said if he was going to be punished for running away, and then be punished for helping to catch runaways, he would choose to be punished for running away. He said that they would not catch him this time, because he had heard that the colonel was very angry at what had happened when Francisco died, and he would not allow another such adventure."

Father Juan thought over all he had learned in the past few days and decided that this was probably a very accurate assessment of how the military would react to this defection. "I am sorry if Tiburcio was punished because of me. As a matter of fact, he didn't really tell me much about that expedition."

Xavier shrugged. "Tiburcio is always looking for a reason to run away, and Father Danti is always looking for a reason to punish the Indians."

"What about you? You have spoken to me, too. Has Father Danti tried to punish you?"

Xavier looked levelly at the monk. "You know, Father, there are Indians who invite punishment from the priests, and there are Indians the priests think very carefully about before they would punish them. We are subject to the orders of the Franciscans, but we are not all willing to be treated as children." He looked carefully at the priest. "Do you understand what I mean?"

"I do, I do indeed," Father Juan answered. He was very aware of the fact that the history of the Franciscans in California was one suffused with cruelty towards the Indians, and that from time to time that cruelty had been repaid by the Indians toward certain missionaries. Various priests at various missions had suffered beatings and even death at the hands of disgruntled neophytes.

"Good evening, Father. I will let you know when I have given Father de Landaeta my petition."

16

Father Juan spent the next several days carefully constructing a report to send to Monterey. In that report, he noted all he had done to date. He gave detailed chronologies and information on the diseases he had so carefully studied. He included summaries of the interviews he had conducted with priests, soldiers, and natives. He explained his rationale for suggesting that San Francisco was home to malaria, which had not been seen so far in any of the other missions. (He was careful to point out the fact that likely that was because no one was looking for it.) He suggested that perhaps a future study might be done to see if this exotic disease was present throughout California. He included his concerns about the as-yet undiagnosed illness that had killed Francisco. He pointed out that, while quite often there were deaths of the natives that could not be explained, none of them occurred with the rapidity that had killed Francisco. If there *was* some disease lurking in San Francisco's damp clime which could, in twenty-four hours, kill an apparently healthy young man, that was something for all to think very carefully about. He pointed out that there had never been known an illness that manifested itself in just one individual. If a sickness could kill one, it could kill others, or even more chilling, all.

Finally, he concluded with his own observations of the climate in San Francisco. He found it depressing and probably unhealthy. He had been told by natives, Franciscans, and soldiers all that it was very localized. If one wanted to travel just thirty or so miles north, east or south, the weather was sunny and warm. Any further to the west, he pointed out, would land one in the Pacific Ocean. His theory was that the huge bay of San Francisco was a natural "trap" for the cold fogs that rolled in off the ocean. He closed with a very tentative suggestion: Perhaps the powers that be might consider relocating San Francisco? Failing that, he ended, he could see only that sickness, disease and unhappiness would continue to plague "Mission Dolores."

He sat back and reviewed his report, not once, but several times. He changed a sentence here or added a word there. In that process, he realized that before he sent this report to his superiors, he should first make a report to one other person. He decided to visit Estella the next day. Looking at the calendar, he noted that the next day was Sunday, which would perhaps be the best day of all to visit her. All of the neophytes had Sunday off, and once her attendance at Mass was over Estella, would be in the village all day. He put the completed report in the single drawer of his writing table and left for evening prayer.

At Mass the next morning he noticed Estella, on the right side of the chapel along with several other neophytes, some women from the town and a few soldiers' wives. As she stood for the dismissal from Mass, he very discreetly signaled to her that he would like to see her after Mass. After taking off his vestments, he walked around the side of the church and to the plaza in the front. Small groups of people stood around the fountain, catching up on the week's activities and gossip. Estella, with her child in its sling, was off to one side. Xavier was visiting with her. He approached them.

"Good morning, Father," they greeted him in unison. Father Juan suddenly remembered Xavier's plans.

"Your petition for emancipation! Did you give it to Father de Landaeta yesterday? I was supposed to write you a recommendation!"

"It is all right, Father; I am going to give it Father de Landaeta today. You can give him your recommendation tonight."

"Good; I will. How are you, Estella? I haven't seen you for several days."

"I am fine, Father." Estella had on the plain garb of the mission neophytes, but she was wearing for Mass a beautiful and finely wrought *mantilla*. It was a soft cream color that accentuated her brown skin, black hair and dark eyes. He noted that her hair was just slightly longer than the standard bob she always wore.

"Estella," he said, "I would like to come and visit you this afternoon, in the village. Would that be all right?"

"Yes, Father, that would be fine. I will arrange for Oralia, or one of the other women, to be there

"Good," he said. "I'll be there about three o'clock this afternoon." He left Estella and Xavier still visiting in the plaza in front of the church.

Later that afternoon he walked down to the village, located just a little way from the edge of the bay. Children ran through the streets and around the outskirts of the little settlement. Groups of people were gathered in front of several of the huts, visiting, weaving baskets or mending fishing nets as they talked and laughed. As he walked into the village, he was greeted by Claudio.

"*Buenas tardes, Padre*. I understand Estella is expecting you. Do you remember which is her hut, or would you like me to have someone take you there?"

"Good afternoon, Claudio. I think I know where Estella's hut is. I will not need an escort there."

Claudio vaguely waved a hand in the direction of Estella's hut. "Have a good afternoon, Father."

Approaching the hut, Father Juan stood in front of the deerskin that covered the opening to the hut's interior, and called out. "Estella, it is Father Juan. I would like to come in and visit with you."

"Come in, Father," Estella called back. Stooping to enter the low opening, he found Estella and Oralia, seated on cushions, with a steaming tea pot on a rock between them.

"Come in, Father," Estella repeated. She rose and, casting a few cushions down, she invited him to join them. Father Juan lowered himself and had barely gotten himself seated when Oralia, wordlessly but with a broad smile, extended a cup of steaming tea to him. They exchanged a few pleasantries, discussed the weather, and commented on the tea. Father Juan commented on her growing hair. Estella cast her eyes down and answered, "I will not cut my hair, until I have been able to properly bury my husband."

He was a bit taken aback and didn't know quite how to respond to this, but he realized that her comment provided him the opening he needed to fully attend to the purpose of his visit.

"Estella," he began hesitatingly, "it is that which I have come to visit with you about. I believe I have completed almost all of the work I was sent here to do. I have learned several new things about the illnesses of the Indians, and I am ready to make a report to the governor."

Her expression changed not at all, as she asked, over the rim of her cup, "Have you found out how Francisco died? Have you discovered where he is buried?"

"I have found out where he is buried. What disease he died from, I do not know, and" he added slowly, "I would not be able to determine that after this time. Also, Father Landaeta does not think it is practical for us to consider returning Francisco's remains to Mission Dolores."

Estella absorbed this information quietly. She took one more sip from her cup and carefully placed it on the mat in front of her. She looked up at Father Juan.

"Thank you, Father," she replied quietly. "Would you like more tea?" She raised the pot towards him.

Father Juan was completely taken aback. He was not sure what sort of reaction he had been expecting, but it certainly had not been a polite inquiry about tea. Sobs, screams, tears; remonstrances in two languages; anything other than an inquiry about tea. He had long held the opinion that he would never, ever, understand the ways of the native people, and this startling question completely buttressed that view.

"Uh...no. Uh...thank you," he stammered. He stared across at the young woman holding the teapot. Any childlike features he had ever seen in her were nowhere in evidence. He was facing a stolid and placid woman—a woman whose outward calm, he knew, was hiding a swirling storm of emotions and feelings. He had thought over the past several months that he had begun to know her. Now he realized that, not only had he never known her, but he never would know her.

There was nothing more he could say. With the vague feeling of a child being dismissed by a parent after some errant deed, Father Juan stood up and began saying his goodbyes. Estella rose to see him out the door. Taking his hand as he stooped to duck through it, she said, once more, *"Gracias, Padre. Buenas noches."*

"Buenas noches, Señora." He escaped to a soft, warm evening and the setting sun. He followed it westward and to the south, back to the mission.

It is done, he thought, as he walked. He still wasn't sure yet just *what* was done. He had told Estella that he was going to send his report to the governor, and that as far as he knew, Francisco had died of an unspecified illness. He had told her that Francisco would remain buried in the *pantanos.* It occurred to him now that what he had told her was exactly what *she* had told *him,* many weeks ago. In short, he had told her nothing she didn't already know, and she had accepted the information with an amazing placidness and almost a complete lack of any further interest. *Somehow,* he thought, *I don't think it is done.*

He returned to his cell to find that a note, written in the unpracticed hand of the neophytes, had been slipped under his door:

Father Juan. I have given the father superior a written request for my release from the mission, and permission to remove myself to the town of Yerba Buena. If you would please give him a letter of favorable recommendation in this matter. Yours, Xavier

The prospect of a new life for the young man who had so much impressed him drove thoughts of all other matters out of his head. He immediately sat down and wrote a glowing letter of recommendation: *He has a demonstrated skill in a trade which is much in demand. He has shown himself to be a faithful son of the church. He has always comported himself in an honest and honorable way.* Finally, he added what he hoped would be an unassailable argument: *He will be a perfect example of the success of our efforts, since one of the objectives of the mission system is to produce faithful, tax-paying subjects for his majesty the king.*

He took the letter immediately to the superior's office. Father de Landaeta was enjoying the evening with a glass of brandy.

"Come in, Juan, please; have a drink with me." He handed him a glass and poured for the younger priest. "What brings you here?"

"I understand, Father, that you have received a petition for emancipation from Xavier." Without waiting for acknowledgement, he handed his own letter to Father de Landaeta. "I would like to have this accompany his petition." The superior took the letter and read it quickly. He looked up and smiled.

"You certainly throw yourself wholeheartedly into whatever you do, Juan. This is more a recommendation for canonization than for emancipation." As Father Juan started to respond the older priest held up the all-too-familiar restraining hand. "Have no fear, Father. Xavier is, as you say, the perfect candidate for emancipation, and I am sure his petition will be granted without difficulty. As you know, that decision is not mine but the father president's and the governor's. I will send his petition and your letter to them tomorrow, along with my personal recommendation for approval. I am sure the next messenger from Monterey will bring very happy news to *Señor* Xavier.

Remind him when you see him that he should be thinking of a surname."

At Father Juan's questioning glance, the superior explained. "When one of the natives decides to convert and be baptized, they are given a Christian name, of course, but none of them has a surname. The natives identify individuals by a name, followed by the tribe or clan they belong to. For instance, 'Toribio of the Miwok.' As long as they are charges of the mission, one name is really all they need. But if Xavier though is going to establish himself as a member of the community of Yerba Buena, he will need a surname to identify himself on legal documents and other things, as he is recognized as a member of the *gente de razón*."

The younger priest continued to stare blankly. "Why, I had never thought of that," he said. "In all of my time in Alta California, although I dealt with many Indians, it never occurred to me that they might have last names. I am sure I must have heard of some, but it just never registered. How does one go about picking a surname? None of us has ever picked one, it was ours from birth, we got it from our fathers or maybe from both parents. If your parents had no last name how do you ever pick one?" he finished his query, with a continued puzzled look.

The superior laughed lightly and told him, "Some of them just pick a name from what they know. There are an amazing number of freed neophytes named 'River' or 'Fox' or 'Coyote.' Some of them adopt a name from one of the soldiers or priests they have known, or perhaps someone they greatly admire." He added, "It has made for some very interesting names."

Putting aside but not resolving his perplexed state of mind as to how one would arrive at a last name, Father Juan decided to tell the superior that he was in the act of finalizing his report to the governor and the father president. He gave him a general overview of what it would contain and the recommendations he was making. He concluded by telling the superior, "I think you can tell Father Danti that his concerns can be put to rest. There is nothing in the material I have investigated so far to suggest that Francisco died of anything other than an illness as he has reported. Father Danti does not need to be bothered with any more troublesome questions from me."

"I am sure he will happy to hear that," Father de Landaeta said.

"I am *sure* he will," Father Ibarra answered.

Still pondering what he had always taken for granted, Father Juan left, promising to get Xavier started on a last name. Since correspondence from San Francisco to Monterey and back again would take, at a minimum, a week or ten days, he felt he had plenty of time to address the issue.

The very next day, though, just to be sure nothing was left to chance, he talked to Xavier about it. The concept that had been so novel to Father Juan had long ago occurred to the young man. "I have been thinking about it, Father. I will decide as soon as my permission is granted."

Father Juan, still intrigued at the concept of choosing your own name, was tempted to ask him what name or names he was considering. He decided that would probably not be appropriate, and so he left Xavier to contemplate his new name. He could not keep himself from musing, though. *If I had the opportunity to choose a totally new name for myself, what name would I choose?* In the meantime, he reminded himself, he had a report to finalize and send to Monterey.

17

While a new name for Xavier would wait for time and circumstances, it was only two days later that he was summoned to the superior's office to discover that certain matters would not wait for anything and would follow their own schedule. As he entered the superior's study, he was greeted not only by Father de Landaeta but by Father Danti.

"Estella is gone," a grim-faced Father de Landaeta advised him.

"I don't understand," Father Juan answered. "Gone? When, to where?"

"That is what we are trying to determine," the superior told him. "She did not appear for work yesterday. It caused us no alarm, because quite often the mothers of young children must tend to the needs of their children..."

Father Danti interrupted. "I have complained of this for a long time. From the time they get pregnant until the child is weaned the Indian women are more trouble than they are worth."

Father Juan could not control himself. "What are you suggesting, Father? That we should not allow them to get pregnant, or once pregnant we should not allow them to deliver, or once delivered we should not allow them to provide a mother's care to their child? Which is it, Antonio, you think would be the best course of action? Let me know, and I will make that recommendation in my next report to the governor!"

"I am simply saying..." Father Danti began, only to be interrupted once again by a trembling Father Juan.

"What you are saying is that a piece of your machinery, who happens to be the mother of a child, is not available to turn out her allotment of fabric for your looms."

"Silence, the two of you," a startlingly authoritative Father de Landaeta ordered. "We are not here to discuss various theories of the role the neophytes play in mission life. We are not here to discuss the role we play in their lives; we are not here to second guess what has happened. We are here to discover exactly when, and how, and most importantly *why* a young mother and an infant in our care have disappeared."

"I will get an expedition together to go after her," Father Danti offered.

Father de Landaeta answered emphatically. "You will not!" He modulated his tone slightly. "I do not think, Antonio, that is what we want to do. For right now I, as the superior of this mission, am expressly forbidding any expedition to be sent after her." Both Father Danti, and Father Ibarra looked intently at the newly assertive Father de Landaeta. He continued. "I want the two of you to talk to the neophytes and those in the village and see what you might learn. Father Antonio, you talk to the neophytes here at the mission. Father Juan, you go to the village and talk to the people there. I want both of you to report back to me by three o'clock this afternoon. I will decide where we go from there."

"Every day we delay going after her, she gets further away, and the further away she gets the less chance we have of catching her," an exasperated Father Danti protested.

Father de Landaeta leaned forward and interlocked the fingers of his hand. He looked intently at Father Danti. "Estella is a Christian member of our community; she is not some prey we are trying to 'catch.' We do not know that she has left of her own accord. She may have been abducted. She may have fallen down a cliff at the beach. All we know is that for two days now, she has not reported for work. When you made inquiries among the neophytes today, as I understand it they simply said, 'She is not here, Father; she has been gone for two days now.' What I am attempting to get is some elaborating information on that very sketchy report. Is that clear, Antonio?"

"Yes, Father," a cowed, but sullen Father Danti answered. Bidding their superior good day, the two priests rose. Father Ibarra hung back, and as the other priest left, he turned back to the superior.

"Father de Landaeta?"

"Yes, Juan?" the haggard superior answered.

"On Sunday, I talked with Estella. I told her in the same general terms as I told you what my report to the governor would say, and that I had found nothing to indicate that Francisco's death was other than as reported by Father Danti and the corporal. I also told her that we did not see it as practical to recover her husband's remains."

"Yes?" the other priest encouraged.

"She received that news in a very strange fashion."

"What do you mean by that?"

"I know she has a strong feeling that her husband did not just get sick and die. I also know that burying him at Mission San Francisco is very important to her. I would have expected her to be angry at my conclusion, or sad, or disbelieving, or...I'm not really sure what."

"And how did she react?" the superior asked.

Father Juan hesitated just a moment and answered. "She asked me if I would like some more tea."

Father de Landaeta could not keep the startled, confused look from his face.

"That was exactly my reaction, Father," Father Juan said. "It was a very strange, almost nonresponsive response," he paused for a second, "if there can be such a thing."

"The natives are a people apart from us," Father de Landaeta offered. "Even though we have been here for more than twenty years, and even though, for those of Estella's age, we have *always* been here, they will tell us only what they think we want to hear. They will talk with us only if it is to their advantage. Estella obviously has her own view of what happened to her husband. She tried to convince you of that view and failed. It is my guess that she is through talking to you." A very tired looking Father de Landaeta closed, "Please, Juan, visit with the villagers and see what you can learn. I will talk with you this afternoon."

Despondent, Father Ibarra left the superior's office. Although Father de Landaeta had seemingly dismissed his comments about Estella's reaction, he began to wonder if she was emotionally stable. He didn't give much credence to the idea that she might have been abducted or "fallen off a cliff," not given the careful watch of her he had seen by the villagers. He was almost certain that she had left of her own accord. What sort of woman would leave the safety of the village life for the dangers of the wilderness, and what sort of woman would willingly expose her infant to those same dangers? He had always seen Estella as an intent, driven, but intelligent young woman, not as an irrational one. Was he completely wrong? Most troubling of all was Father de Landaeta's assertion: "She is through talking to you."

He stopped briefly at his cell to gather a small pouch, his staff and a sombrero, and arrived in the village in the late morning. It surprised him that the village was almost deserted, a few old men and old women who stared at him as he walked into their midst. He realized that the younger people would be at work in the mission fields or shops. Even the children had chores or religious classes to attend. He noticed Oralia, the woman who had served as Estella's "chaperone" on his first visit. He approached her.

"Oralia, you are Estella's friend. I think you know I am Estella's friend as well. I need to know, where is Estella? Where has she gone? We are worried about her safety."

Oralia looked at the priest and replied simply. "Estella has gone to find her husband, Father." She turned to an older man who was watching their conversation. "Castano. Please, join the Father and me."

The old man joined them and suggested they go to his hut to talk. Settling down with the inevitable pot of tea the old man began talking. "I am Castano, Father. I have known Estella since the day she was born. I knew her mother and father, and I have considered her my daughter since they died. I was very happy for her when she married Francisco, and now..." his voice trailed off. "Estella told me of her plan to find Francisco's remains. I did not think it was a good idea. I and Oralia are Estella's two closest friends. We both asked her not to do it, but she said that if Francisco was to return to Mission San Francisco, it was she who must return him; no one else would."

Suppressing a surge of guilt, Father Juan spoke. "Estella asked me to help her find Francisco's remains. I refused to do that. I did not realize how important that was to her. If we can find her, I will help her accomplish that. I know now that she will not rest until that is done. I will help her bring him back to San Francisco. Now, unfortunately, before I can help Estella find her husband, I must first find Estella."

18

As planned, the three priests met that afternoon in Father de Landaeta's office. The superior began the meeting.

"Antonio, have you had any new information from any of the neophytes?"

Father Danti gave a disgusted snort. "The only information I have been able to get is, 'I know nothing, Father.' Sometimes they'll elaborate upon that by reassuring me, 'Oh, I do not talk to any of the women, Father, I know that is forbidden. I know nothing of what a single woman may have done.'"

Father de Landaeta turned to Father Ibarra. "Juan?"

"I have been told that Estella did not come to the mission to work on Monday."

"We already knew that!" Father Danti interjected.

"But," Father Juan continued purposefully, "she did come to the mission Monday night, when all of us were asleep."

"But why?" Father de Landaeta asked.

"She came to the mission, specifically to the church, to pray to *San Miguel*." He reminded the other two priests, "We have taught the neophytes that one of the duties Saint Michael performs is to lead the souls of the dead from their resting place, to heaven. Estella asked Saint Michael to lead her to the place where her husband rests, and then she left, trusting Saint Michael." He paused and then continued carefully, "She left to find her husband."

It was several seconds before the other two could comment.

"How ridiculous!" was Father Danti's observation. "Her husband is dead!"

"What faith!" was the quiet observation of Father de Landaeta.

Father Juan commented, "Ridiculousness or faith, it is a lesson to all of us that the Indians do not always make a distinction between doctrinal truths and interesting legends when we are talking to them about the faith. Their own beliefs have always been that a person who dies just goes on to another life, so Saint Michael, wandering about, leading souls to their eternal reward, is a very logical, reassuring concept, and one not at all hard for them to accept."

"Theology aside," Father de Landaeta said, "what should we do now?"

"Why, go and bring her back," Father Danti exclaimed. "We need to bring her back before...we need to bring her back!"

"We do have her safety, and the safety of the child, to consider." Father de Landaeta observed.

"Let me offer some more information I got from the villagers," Father Ibarra suggested. "They are not concerned about her safety. Estella had told certain of the villagers what she was planning. As soon as they knew, they began sending messengers out to all of the surrounding countryside. They have since been hearing back from the people all around the bay. She had no trouble getting a boatman to take her across the bay. He took her all the way to the smaller bay, San Pablo, and the mouth of the Rio San Joaquin. He asked her if she wanted him to go further with her and she said no. He had heard of her husband's death and he asked her how she was going to find where he is buried. She said that she had talked to some of the Indians who were there when her husband died, and they told her how many leagues from the river it was, how many curves of the river they had passed, how far from the woods, etc. She said San Miguel would lead her to her husband. Her people and the neighboring clans will all be watching out for her. They will help her, and they will shelter her and the child and be sure she travels safely."

Father Danti could not wait to once again suggest, "We can find out who took her across the bay. We can make him take us, as well. We can make him take us to right where he left her. We can have caught up with her early tomorrow morning. A woman traveling with a child cannot travel very quickly. We can have her back in the mission by Wednesday evening, or Thursday at the latest. Then we can teach her that she is not free to just go wandering about following Saint Michael or anyone else."

"There is more I learned," Father Ibarra continued. "Estella took very much to heart our teachings about the Communion of Saints. She accepts that we, the living and the dead, will all be rejoined one day. She looks forward to that day." He paused here and added dramatically, "If we try to stop her from finding her husband, she will hasten the arrival of that day for herself, her husband, and their child." At the intense looks of puzzlement on the faces of the other two priests, he explained. "She will kill herself, and her child, before we can take her back to the mission."

Father Danti scoffed. "All of these Indians are always planning some dramatic gesture. This is not the first time I have heard of one who said, 'Oh, Father, if you don't allow me to marry so-and-so I'll kill myself,' or, 'If you don't let me go off to the mountains to gather acorns I'll die.' None of them ever has yet."

"You may be right, Antonio," Father Ibarra said. "I am not sure, though, that we are dealing with a rational person. We are dealing with a woman consumed with grief, long after the period when we would have expected her to recover." He decided to add, "I would hate to have another expedition end in the death of not just one, but two neophytes—one of them an infant."

The look on Father Danti's face showed that he found the comment highly offensive, even insulting. He made no response, however.

Father de Landaeta sighed, leaned back in his chair, and shook his head slowly. "I will not have the blood of this lady and of her child on my hands," he declared.

"It would not be on your hands, Father," Father Danti suggested. "Whatever other lessons of her catechism Señora Estella may have learned, she has obviously forgotten the fifth commandment."

Father de Landaeta's incredulous stare brought an uncomfortable silence on the group. Finally, he asked, "Juan, what do you suggest? I cannot just leave her wandering around in the *pantanos*, no matter how much the natives are watching out for her. We cannot send an expedition after her without great danger. What do you suggest?"

"I have given this much thought, Father, since I visited with the villagers. Estella will not be satisfied until she is able to bury whatever remains of her husband in holy ground."

Father Danti leaned forward and gave a peremptory query. "What *would* remain of her husband after a year or so?"

"Very little," Father Juan replied. "As I understand it, where Francisco was buried was a very moist, almost swamp-like area. In ground such as that, and particularly with no covering other than a blanket, decomposition would be very rapid. At best, all that might remain now would be skeletal remains with perhaps desiccated tissue. Perhaps some pieces of clothing, certainly shoes. It would not be a pleasant sight." Father Danti sat back.

Father Juan continued. "As you have said, Father," he turned his remarks to the superior, "to send an expedition after her could have very unfortunate consequences. We might, though, be able to send some trusted persons, some persons she considers friends, to try to talk with her, and to convince her that we will at least help her find her husband."

Both of the other priests asked almost the same question. "Who would those trusted friends be?"

"She has a very close friend named Oralia. If anyone could convince Estella to let us help her, she could. There is also an old man in the village named Castano, who is practically a father to her and whose judgments she values and," here he paused and took a deep breath, "I think she still trusts me."

"You?" Father Danti asked incredulously. "You and two *Indios* are going to go wandering through the swamps looking for a deranged woman who herself is looking for a body that has been buried a year? *Fantastico*! A week later we will be sending a party out to find you."

Father de Landaeta leaned back. "I will have to think about this. I will let you know. It is time for Vespers." He rose, and before they left for the church he reminded them, "There will be no expedition, no matter how it is structured, without my express permission."

It wasn't until after evening prayer, and night prayer as well, that Father de Landaeta called Father Juan aside. "Juan, meet with me if you would in my office." Father Danti noticed the other two priests walking away together but simply made his way to his own cell.

Settling into the chair behind his desk the superior began. "I have given much thought and prayer to what we are facing, and to what you have suggested. Tomorrow, if you can, I want you to take the people you mentioned from the village and see if you can find Estella and convince her to return."

"*Gracias, Padre, gracias.* I think we can do that. I will go to the village first thing in the morning. Could you arrange to have a canoe take us across the bay? As Father Danti said, if we have several strong men to paddle it, we can get across the bay very quickly."

The superior nodded.

"I will not need the men once I get to the mouth of the *San Joaquin*, and I can arrange to have a signal fire when we are ready to come back across. I hope it will be just a day or two." He paused for a bit and then asked, "There is one other thing I would ask you to do, Father."

"What is that?" the superior asked.

"I have been thinking about this ever since we last talked. As I said, I think if I take Oralia and Castano I will be able to talk to Estella without alarming her. But we cannot forget that our objective is different than Estella's."

"What are you saying, Juan?"

"Our objective is to get Estella and her child safely back to the mission. Estella's objective is to find her husband and bring him back to the mission. On her own, she will never be able to accomplish that. No matter what descriptions the Indians have given her, she is going to do little other than wander around a huge and, if I understand it, largely featureless landscape. If the grave was marked at all, it was with a wooden cross, and that cross is undoubtedly gone after a winter of rain, wind and a rising river."

"Then what can we do?" Father de Landaeta asked. "You yourself have just described her objective as impossible."

"It is impossible for her to accomplish, and it is impossible for me to accomplish. It may, however, be very possible for one particular man to accomplish." At the superior's questioning look he explained. "One of the soldiers, a Private Galindo, constructed very detailed maps of the route of that expedition, including the burial site. He is perhaps the best soldier they have at land navigation. If he can accompany us and use the maps he drew, I think the task will be much easier."

"Now you are talking about involving the military again. I thought we wanted to avoid that."

"That is what I want to ask you to consider. I want you to convince the colonel (*to convince the lieutenant to convince the sergeant to convince the corporal,* he thought to himself,) to let us take Private Galindo with us. Not as a soldier, but simply as a young man doing the *padres* a favor and leading Father Juan to the place where Francisco is buried. Then we could achieve both objects.

We will find Francisco and convince Estella to come back to the mission to properly bury him."

"You know, Juan," Father de Landaeta told him with a slight smile, "I told you some time ago that I did not feel as if I was suited to the duties of superior. In the past several days, you have certainly introduced me to a whole range of duties I have never even contemplated. I must say, though: they have been interesting ones." He gave a slight sigh. "I will go to the *presidio* in the morning and talk to Colonel Alberni. He and I regularly spend a night at cards and brandy. He is very good at brandy, and I am very good at cards. The colonel owes me a favor or two. You go to the village in the morning I will go to the *presidio* and we will meet at the landing below the *presidio* at nine o'clock. I think Private Galindo and his map will be there. *Buenas noches, Juan.*"

Father Juan retired that night full of anticipation for the adventure that would begin in the morning. He was too full of plans and possible scenarios to sleep. He walked over to the church. Just before entering, he glanced back to the dark shadow that was the bay, and to the darkness on the other side. Somewhere in that darkness was Estella. He went into the church through a side door and walked up to the statue of San Jose, in a small niche to the left of the altar. Ah! St. Joseph, of course. He knelt in front of the statue. *St. Joseph,* he prayed, *you protected Mary and the baby Jesus in the desert on the flight into Egypt. Protect your daughter Estella and her baby in the wilderness tonight.*

¤ 19

Father Juan left early the next morning, right after Lauds, for the village. He didn't even bother to have breakfast. It was a gray, overcast morning as he started out. He realized just how early he had left when, on arriving at the village, he found just a few women stirring about, beginning the fires in their outdoor ovens.

He asked for Claudio, and one of the women went off to find him. The *alcade* shortly came up to the priest, obviously still trying to force himself fully awake.

"Buenas dias, Padre," he said to the priest, and then immediately turned to the woman standing by the fire and muttered to her. He moved closer to the warmth of the fire in the brick oven and motioned to the priest to do the same.

"What is it I can do for you, Father, *so early in the morning*?"

The priest grinned apologetically. "I am sorry, Claudio, to disturb the village so early. I am going to see if I can find Estella, and to help her find her husband's remains."

At the quizzical look of the *alcalde*, he continued. "It will be just me and one young soldier who has a map of where they buried Francisco. No other soldiers will be with us. I am hoping that Castano and Oralia will accompany me. They should be able to convince Estella that we mean her no harm. It is that I have come to see you about."

Just as Claudio began to answer, the woman he had spoken to approached them and handed the *alcalde* and the priest tin mugs of steaming coffee. They stood for a while in the chill morning air, sipping the strong coffee. Finally, the *alcalde* spoke.

"My authority as *alcalde* is the authority of the Franciscans. I have little authority to tell my people to do other things, and especially those who remain unconverted, which Castano and Oralia are. We will ask them." He turned again to the woman tending her fire and spoke a few words to her. She called to two of the children who were beginning to move about, and sent them off to speak to Castano and Oralia. Claudio and Father Juan stood, sipping their coffee and watching the village come to life. One of the children came back.

Father Juan addressed him in Spanish. "Did you speak with Castano, *hijo*?"

"*Sí, Padre*, I woke him up and told him you wanted him to accompany you on an expedition to the *pantanos*."

"And what did he say, *hijo*?"

"He said, 'Now?' and then he turned over and went back to sleep." The priest and *alcalde* grinned at each other. "I will get him," Claudio said, and walked off to the circle of huts. Finally, both Castano and Oralia joined the growing group around the fire.

Father Juan looked at his watch and realized he had indeed been anxious to start his trip. It was just a little after six o'clock. He remembered that Father de Landaeta had said he would meet him at nine o'clock, so there was really no hurry to be off. The group found seats around the fire and had a breakfast of corn cakes and coffee. Father Juan explained in detail to both Castano and Estella, and to the ever-increasing crowd of villagers gathering to listen, what he was asking of them.

"How many soldiers are you taking?" Oralia asked warily.

"I am not taking any soldiers," Father Juan answered, and then added, "There will be no military on this expedition. Actually, I *am* taking one young man from the *presidio*, but he will not be there as a soldier. He will be there only as a mapmaker. He knows where Francisco is buried, and he made a map of that place. He will be able to take us to that spot. He *is* a soldier, but I assure you, he will not be traveling as a soldier and he will have no weapons."

Castano and Oralia discussed this information between themselves. Castano spoke. "We are not sure what to do. We do not want to have anything to do with any soldiers. A soldier is a soldier, and even if he does not have any weapons, his comrades do. We do not trust the soldiers. We do, though, want to find Estella. We worry about her. She would not let us talk her out of going, and neither would she hear of us accompanying her."

Father Juan pleaded, "I think without your help I have no real hope of getting Estella to come back with me, and without this young man we have no real hope of finding Francisco's grave. Can I ask you, please, to at least start out with me on this trip? If at any time you do not like what is taking place, you can leave. Indeed, how could I stop you?"

Again, the two conversed. Castano spoke to Father Juan. "We will go with you on this expedition, but we will leave it any time we wish."

"*Bueno, bueno*," Father Juan agreed, "yes, anytime you want you may leave. You do not need to even worry about me. If you decide to leave, I will have the mapmaker" — he consciously avoided the word 'soldier' — "guide me back to the mission. I just want to have you along to talk to Estella if...when we find her."

"When do you want to start?" Claudio asked.

"This morning," Father Juan said. He looked at his watch. "We are to meet the mapmaker, to begin crossing the bay in about one hour." Claudio and Castano looked questioningly toward the bay but said nothing.

Castano and Oralia left to gather items for their journey. Claudio instructed the women to prepare some corncakes and gourds full of water for the travelers to take. He and Father Juan sat by the fire to await the return of the other two. The day was fully light now, but still gray and damp with the fog overhead.

When the two Indians had returned, they all rose and, with a series of farewell to the villagers, began the walk toward the *presidio*. They were able to get to the landing without going through the *presidio* grounds itself, much to the relief of the two nervous Indians. As they approached the small pier, Father Juan noticed Father de Landaeta and several other people standing there. He did not see Private Galindo.

"*Buenas dias, Juan,*" Father de Landaeta greeted him.

"Good morning, Father," the other priest answered. He looked around nervously. "Where is Private Galindo, is he not coming?"

"He is over there," the superior answered, pointing to a group at the end of the pier. As Father Juan peered at the figures one of them swept from his head a battered sombrero and waved to him. Private Galindo was totally unrecognizable in pair of cotton trousers, brown shirt and sombrero. This was better than he had hoped for. Father de Landaeta put a hand on his arm and pulled him a little closer.

"I must tell you, Juan, that Colonel Alberni has *serious* misgivings about this. He is still hearing complaints from Monterey about the expedition last year. He does not want the slightest hint made that he is sending even one of his soldiers on an expedition to return runaways. Private Galindo has been given leave from the *presidio* to accompany you on a purely volunteer basis. Should anything happen to Private Galindo when he is on this trip, the army will not be responsible."

"I understand," Father Juan answered. "I will watch out for him."

The young soldier had walked up from the pier and now joined them. He was smiling and ebullient. "*Buenas dias, Padre,*" he greeted Father Juan.

"Good morning, Private. Are you ready to begin our trip?"

"Oh yes, Father, I am ready, but," he gestured to the group at the end of the pier, "they are not."

"What do you mean?" Father Juan asked.

"The *Indios* who are going to take us across the bay say we cannot leave until this afternoon. They say the current is running out to the ocean, and if we try to cross now, we will be swept out to sea. They say we must wait until afternoon when the current turns, and then we can go across."

Father Juan looked out at what appeared to be a featureless stretch of water. "I don't see any current, and I don't want to wait until this afternoon! It has been several days already, we must leave this morning." He looked questioningly at the father superior.

"Juan, I would advise you to listen to the *Indios* on this matter. They have been sailing on this bay for hundreds of years. They know things about it that we do not. If you try to leave now, you are likely to find yourself washing up on *Los Farralones*, if you are lucky. *Los Farralones*, I am told, are home to great *tiburones*. I advise you to just wait. If you drown, or worse, if you get eaten by *los tiburones blancos*, you will never find Estella, and she will never find her husband."

Unhappily, Father Juan agreed. He went down to the Indians who were preparing two canoes, and asked them exactly what time they would be leaving. Two o'clock seemed the best guess. One of them told him that he was the one who had taken the neophyte woman across two days ago. She had wanted to go to Rio San Joaquin. He would take them to where he had left her, but he was insistent that they could not leave now and must wait until the tides and currents changed. Father Juan decided to return to the mission with Father de Landaeta. Private Galindo decided to take advantage of his brief respite from military discipline and spend a few hours exploring Yerba Buena. Father Juan explained to Oralia and Castano what was happening. They decided to go back to the village and promised to return in plenty of time for the afternoon departure.

Immediately after the noon meal, although it was still early, Father Juan headed back to the landing. The sun was shining now and the walk down to the bay was a pleasant and warm one. None of the other of the party was back at the pier. He pulled his breviary from the folds of his robe and, settling himself on the dock with his back against a piling, he began reading.

He had had a largely sleepless night, and soon the warm sunshine, gentle rocking of the pier, and soothing lap of the water lulled him to sleep. Footsteps clattering on the boards woke him up. Private Galindo had just stepped onto the pier. The monk furtively picked up the prayer book lying carelessly in his lap.

"Good afternoon, Private. Pull up a pier and visit with me while we wait."

Private Galindo sat cross legged on the boards and told him of his exploration of the town of Yerba Buena. He had never seen it in full daylight, his previous visits being limited to a few nighttime forays with some of his comrades after duty hours. Father Juan did not press for further explanation of what those nighttime forays might have involved. He asked him what he thought of the town.

"Very hilly, very steep. They build their houses right on the side of the hills. I don't know how they keep them from sliding down. But, very pretty, growing fast, will soon be bigger than Monterey," the young man ventured. Father Juan asked him for his understanding of the expedition they were planning.

"*Si, Padre*," he answered. "I think I know. You want me to show you where we buried the *Indio* who died on the expedition last year." He patted a leather pouch at his side. "I have my maps here; I can find his grave."

"That is true," Father Juan answered, "that is what we want. We probably will need you to help us do one other thing first. The widow of Francisco has gone out a few days ago and is herself looking for his grave. I want you to help us find her."

"*Si*, crazy *Indio* woman. They mentioned that."

"She is a woman consumed with grief, Private. I am not sure she is crazy. She has beliefs, both Catholic and otherwise, that make it important to her to find her husband. She believes she will find him with the help of God and *San Miguel*. She has an infant with her, and I fear for their safety in the wilds. I think if we help her find her husband, she will come back to the mission with us. You must understand, Private, that we are hoping to find her husband's remains, now probably just a skeleton, and bring them back with us to the mission. Does that bother you?"

The soldier's wide-eyed stare told the priest that it did bother him, but he answered hesitantly, "N-no, Father. If you will bless the skeleton, I will help bring it back."

"Private," the priest asked, "I understand you are doing this on your own, and not as one of your duties as a soldier. I cannot spend the next several days calling you 'Private;' what is your name?"

Without hesitation or emphasis, the young man answered simply. "My name is Miguel, Father. You should call me Miguel."

20

As Father Juan was contemplating the uncanny congruence of the young soldier's name and the task they were asking him to accomplish, Oralia and Castano returned to the pier. The priest introduced everyone. Guarded nods of acknowledgement were exchanged. The awkward silence on the pier was mercifully broken when the two boatmen showed up. They explained that each of them would take two passengers in a canoe. It was decided that Father Juan and Miguel would be in one canoe, while Castano and Oralia would cross in the other. Father Juan and Miguel dropped into the canoes some bundles and tools they had brought.

The boatmen settled their passengers into the canoes, which seemed to the wary priest to be little more than bundles of reeds bound together. They cautioned all against standing or even moving while they were on the water and, taking their own positions, pushed off from the pier.

They were barely out from the pier when they began paddling furiously. Father Juan noticed that they were headed, not across the bay, but seemingly straight out the narrow inlet toward the ocean. He cautiously turned to the oarsman behind him and shouted, "*Contra Costa, contra costa,*" all the time pointing furiously at the opposite shoreline. The man just smiled and nodded. "*Si, si,*" he said, while never slacking his furious strokes and steadfastly heading towards the ocean. Nothing Father Juan said or did would dissuade him from his course. Realizing that all he was going to accomplish was to upset the canoe, the furious priest sat back and resigned himself to going wherever the Indians decided to take him.

They continued on what seemed to be a course to what Father de Landaeta had referred to earlier as *Los Farralones,* until they were more than halfway across the narrow isthmus and almost abreast of what the priest knew were the headlands that defined the entrance to the bay. Suddenly both of the Indians stopped paddling and sat back on their haunches. The canoes briefly continued forward, came to a halt and then began drifting backward — backward and toward the opposite shore! Father Juan watched in amazement as the canoe, with only an occasional correction from one of the paddlers, continued toward the opposite shore. He looked back at the man he had been gesticulating to, who was now smiling broadly. "*Corriente,*" he said, making a wide, sweeping gesture in the air with his paddle, to indicate how the current would carry them. The canoe slipped between the headlands to the left and *Los Islos Angeles* to the right, and continued up a huge inlet of the bay.

Now the oarsmen had to resume paddling again, but with a decidedly more relaxed tempo than they had employed crossing the strait. After they had been paddling for several hours, they entered a narrow arm of the bay and approached what seemed to a limitless horizon of reeds. To Father Juan, the reeds were just an unbroken wall of indistinguishable brown rushes. It was obvious, though, that the Indians were searching for something, and Miguel was glancing from his maps to the shorelines and back to the maps again. Finally, the lead oarsman pointed with his paddle and they proceeded up a still narrower waterway. *"Rio San Joaquin,"* the oarsman said. He dipped a hand into the water and licked his palm, motioning to Father Juan to do the same. When he did, the monk tasted muddy, brackish water, and did not understand what he was accomplishing. Miguel pointed it out to him.

"It is not salty, Father, it is fresh. We are out of the bay and in the river."

Father Juan thoughtfully repeated the experiment. Although he was sure that "fresh" would not have been the descriptor he used, it definitely was not salty.

The waterway continued to narrow and branch off endlessly. Nevertheless, the Indians seemed to know exactly where they were going. Finally, just as it was growing dark, they pulled into the marshy shore and the oarsman indicated that this was where they would stop for the night. They dragged the canoes up on the bank and after securing them, walked still higher up. While the others began arrangements to cook a meal, one of the men led Father Juan a little further on. He pointed to a recent, blackened circle of stones.

"This is where we camped with the woman, Estella. We spent the night with her and her child here. The next day she went that way," he pointed vaguely eastward, "and we returned to *Yerba Buena*. We will do the same now. We will spend the night with you. Tomorrow you go in search of the woman and we will go back to *Yerba Buena*. When you are ready to come back, go to the mouth of the river and light a signal fire. Make it very smoky—use damp reeds once the fire is going and they will make smoke. When we see the smoke from your fire, we will come and take you back across the bay."

They returned to join the group where several small fires had been started and dry rushes spread out into two separate sleeping areas, one for the monk and the soldier, the other for the Indians. Despite his frustration at the prospect of leaving Estella to one more night in the wilderness, Father Juan realized that it would be impossible to proceed in the dark. After a meager meal of corncakes and coffee, they threw green reeds onto the fires, in the hopes that the smoke would keep the clouds of mosquitoes at bay. It was now fully dark, and from the surrounding river and marshes came a crescendo of croaks and squeals. Occasionally there would be a splash and the sounds of some frantic struggle in the water. Father Juan had no idea what sort of creatures lurked out in that damp darkness. The Indians, rolled up in their blankets, seemed totally unconcerned, so he devoted his thoughts to some silent prayers and sleep.

Try as he might, though, he could not sleep. The ground was not hard, but no matter how he turned, it seemed as if something poked him, and the mosquitoes were unbelievably persistent at getting under the blanket that he had pulled over his head. If he pulled it too tight he couldn't breathe, and if he relaxed it just a bit the mosquitoes buzzed around his face and ears. *Do mosquitoes not have to sleep, too?* he wondered.

It was still dark when he decided he was never going to sleep. He achingly rose to his feet and moved closer to the still-smoldering fire. At least here the mosquitoes were not so thick. He paced fitfully around the fire and wondered how soldiers, who spent many nights like this, could stand it. *My cell is sparse by any standard, and my bed is hard, but it is one hundred times more comfortable than this!*

Finally, when the sun rose over the reeds, Private Galindo arose, took his map case, and walked off. "I will be back shortly, Father," he reassured the priest.

Slowly the others began to stir. The boatmen went down to their canoes and, pulling in a slender line they had left out all night, brought up a flopping fish. They poked up one of the smoldering fires, and after killing the fish and gutting it they put it on a plank to the fire's side. Castano brought out a battered pot and boiled water for coffee, Oralia distributed some of the corncakes. Just as they were sitting down to their breakfast, Miguel returned. He joined them in the meal, and as he was finishing his coffee, asked the boatmen, "This is where you left the woman and the baby?"

"*Si, venga,*" one of the boatmen answered, and led him to the same fire ring he had shown Father Juan. Miguel looked carefully around, walked a few paces, turned back, walked a few more, turned back and finally walked off in one direction, where he disappeared in the reeds. Shortly he returned and joined the group around the fire.

"I can see her trail. The reeds make it very easy to track someone." He added without any hint of contempt, "Even you would be able to follow her, Father."

"Where are we with reference to Francisco's grave?" Father Juan asked. Here the young man stepped back from the fire a bit and laid his map case on the ground. He extracted two documents. One, Father Juan recognized as the one Miguel had made of the site of the battle on Father Danti's expedition. The other he had never seen before. It was this drawing that Miguel pointed to first.

"This is a map that I did this morning, when I left the camp for a while. I climbed a high tree so I could use the mountains to the east as landmarks. We are here," he drew a small circle and put an *x* in it. He laid the two maps with their edges aligned. Father Juan was amazed to see that contours of what was labeled "*R. San Joaquin*" on each map came very close to alignment.

"You see Francisco's grave here, and we are here," the young man continued. There was a straight line between the two points, one almost directly above the other. "About one day of marching."

"*Se Bueno!*" interjected Father Juan, "that is not too far away."

Miguel gave a slight sigh, "But first..."

"But first what?" the impatient priest asked.

"First we must find the cra... Indian woman."

"But you said her trail is easy to follow."

"That is true. It will not be hard to find her." Here he paused. "But she is not walking towards her husband's grave. She is walking *away* from it. She is walking in this direction," and he pointed to the mountain ranges on the edge of the map. He continued, "She will keep walking this way until she comes to the great valley; she cannot turn to the south and she will not turn to the north."

"Why is that?" the now thoroughly confused priest asked.

"She cannot turn to the south, because she—and we—are on the north shore of the river. She cannot cross the river without a boat." The two boatmen who had been watching the conversation with interest nodded their heads.

"*Verdad,*" one of them muttered.

"She will not turn to the north because, as you can see," he pointed to the maps, "the river, as it prepares to empty into the bay, takes many separate ways." He held out both hands with the fingers widely spread. "Some of these branches a person could easily wade across, but a person walking without guidance through this country will stay on dry ground. They will not wade through water unless they have a particular reason to. The north bank of the river is the highest and driest ground." Again, the boatmen nodded their heads. "She will just keep walking, where it is easiest to walk, and the river will lead her to the great valley. Before it does that," he pointed once more to the maps, "as you can see, it will take her in a very deep loop to the south. If she succeeds in walking to the great valley," he shrugged, "who knows where she will go, or what will happen to her. The people of the great valley are much more warlike than the *Indios* you are used to, Father."

"How long will it take her to get to the great valley?" the priest asked in some alarm.

Miguel shrugged. "A week, ten days, two weeks? That is not a fear, Father, that she will stumble into the great valley. If we set off after her today, we should find her by the end of today, certainly tomorrow at the latest. She is a woman traveling with an infant. She will not travel very fast. The problem is that every step she takes, and every step we take to follow her, takes us further and further from her husband's grave, which right now is only about five leagues away."

Father Juan thought carefully about all of this. He had hoped to make a quick trip, one or two, at most three days, and return with Estella and with Francisco's remains. Now, they had been gone two days already, they had still not found Estella, and it seemed as if no matter how close she might be, they were probably at least three more days away from her husband's grave. He was absolutely without an idea of how he should proceed. Miguel interrupted his musings.

"Let me suggest something, Father."

"Please do," the anxious priest responded. Every one of the little party was staring at the young man as he explained.

"I understand, Father, that you are the leader of this expedition and I am here only to follow your orders. I think, though, we have a situation that reaches more toward my training as a soldier, than your training as a priest."

Father Juan did not hesitate to interrupt. "Believe me, Miguel, I have no argument with that. You may only be a private, but right now, as far as I am concerned, you are the general in charge of this campaign. Please let me know what you think."

The young soldier smiled broadly. "*Generale*, you say? Will you write a letter to the corporal saying that?"

Without waiting for an answer he continued, still smiling. "Let me suggest that we send the boatmen on their way. We do not need their services until we want to cross the bay again, and right now that is several days away. Most of our traveling now will be on land. The more of us traveling, the slower we will travel. Believe me, a squad can travel much faster than a platoon."

Although he wasn't sure of exactly what the configurations of those two units were, Father Juan was not at all prepared to interfere with the military logic.

"I suggest that you and Castano stay here for at least another night," Private Galindo continued. "Meanwhile, I and the *Indio* woman begin searching for Estella on our own." As Father Juan prepared to object, the young man explained, "As I understand it, she is a good friend of Estella, and the whole reason for bringing her along is that she is the person who will most be able to convince her to come with us. Also, she is young."

Oralia was following Miguel's conversation closely. She frowned at his final comment. Miguel continued. "We want to find Estella as quickly as possible. I intend to march very hard in pursuit of her. He," he gestured to the older Indian, "is old; he will not be able to keep up. You, Father Juan, are not old, but I think you are more fitted to a life of study than a life of marching. You will not be able to keep up either. She is young and she will be able to keep up. In fact," he added as an afterthought, "she can probably march faster than I, for longer." He looked at Father Juan. "I can find Estella but only she," he pointed to Oralia, "can convince her to come back."

Father Juan considered all he had just heard and answered levelly. "First, 'she' has a name. She is Oralia." The young soldier blushed but remained silent. "Second, I do not think she will trust you alone in the wilds."

"*Padre*," Oralia spoke, "I think what he says makes sense. I do not know for sure that Estella will listen to me if I tell her to come back, but I do know for sure that she will not listen to anyone else, and certainly not a Spanish soldier, even if he is not in uniform. I will trust him, Father, because I have seen that you trust him, and Estella has told me that you are a man who can be trusted. And," she couldn't resist adding with a tight-lipped grin, "he is right, I can march faster and longer than he can."

Father Juan gave a resigned sigh. "He too has a name. His name is Miguel. Miguel, may I introduce you to Oralia; Oralia, this is Miguel. There, you two have been formally introduced. You may consider me as your chaperone. I am responsible for each of you and each of you will answer to me for your behavior on this expedition. I expect each of you to put aside any differences you have, and concentrate all of your energies on finding and returning Estella. *Comprende*?" The two young people exchanged a glance, one that Father Juan could not totally interpret, but which he decided was not overtly hostile.

"*Si, Padre*," was the joint reply.

There was further discussion on several points, but finally there was agreement. The boatmen pushed their canoes into the water and turned back downstream. As they disappeared around a bend, Father Juan turned to Miguel.

"Miguel, do you know where the 'mouth of the river' is?"

"Of course, Father, I can get us there very easily," he answered with a puzzled look.

"Good, good," the monk answered.

The four of them returned to their campsite. Castano and Father Juan set about building some lean-tos for a bit more shelter, and gathering more reeds to sleep on. Oralia and Miguel began packing some simple pouches to take on their trip. Miguel insisted on drawing yet another map, this one to show Father Juan how to get back to the mouth of the river, "just in case anything went wrong."

"Nothing will go wrong, Father," he assured the worried priest, "but in the army we always have what we call a *contingencia* ready."

As she and Miguel got ready to embark on their trek, Oralia turned back to the arrangements being made by Father Juan and Castano. "Don't forget to prepare a lean-to for Estella and the baby."

As the two young people disappeared in the reeds, Father Juan and Castano turned back to their chores. Father Juan, as he went about his tasks, said a silent prayer to Saint Christopher to keep the young travelers safe. At one point he noticed Castano taking a small part of the reeds they were gathering and leaving them in a separate pile. He did the same with the branches they used for supports and the cattails they pulled apart for cushioning.

"Castano," he asked, pointing to the pile, "what are those for?" The old man looked at him with a slightly apologetic grin.

"Those are for the gods, Father. I take a part of all we gather and offer it to the gods, in thanksgiving for having provided them to us and for the safety of the young people on their travels."

The monk thought carefully of this. He offered prayers to a God and saints he could not prove existed. Castano offered wood and vegetation to gods he could not prove existed. Very briefly he entertained the thought, *I wonder which one of us is right?* His conscience shouted, *Blasphemy!* and he immediately offered a prayer of contrition.

The day went by very slowly. In the early afternoon the two of them walked down to the river and put out some fishing lines. They walked back to the campsite and relaxed in the sun. They waited for the return of Miguel and Oralia. They waited for darkness. Darkness came, and the two young people had not returned.

21

Several miles upstream, Oralia and Miguel were making their own preparations for the night. They had marched steadily all day, pausing not even for lunch. Oralia had introduced Miguel to the roots of certain of the reeds as a very filling snack that could be munched as they went. Here and there were berries that could be grabbed by the handful. The day was warm and their pace a strenuous one; at almost every opportunity, they would scoop up handfuls of water and splash them over their heads. Once, Oralia tried to convince Miguel to coat his face with a foul-smelling concoction she had brought from the village "to keep the mosquitoes from him." He couldn't bring himself to do that, and soon his face and arms were grotesquely swollen with bites on bites. Oralia had not hesitated to use the solution herself, and clearly she suffered far less from the indignities of the persistent insects.

The only times they stopped were so that Miguel could periodically update his maps. Oralia asked him about them. He explained them to her, pointing to features on the landscape, and then the scribblings on his paper. Her eyes widened with interest. After that, she was engaged each time he stopped to sketch, glancing over his shoulder and once even suggesting that a particularly large tree should be added. Their conversation was generally limited by their blistering pace to that which was exactly necessary. "This way." "Look out." "Careful here." Estella's trail was indeed very clear to both of them. By some unspoken arrangement, they took turns leading, sometimes Miguel, sometimes Oralia. As the sun began setting, Oralia suggested, "We should find a place to stop for the night."

Miguel had no hesitancy in saying with a grin, "I thought you would never say that."

"And you couldn't have?" she asked innocently.

They found a level spot, somewhat distant from the river and the mosquitoes, and began preparing a campsite. As they stood surveying the ground, they glanced quickly at each other. What Miguel saw was a mud-covered, disheveled, wild-haired creature. What Oralia saw was a red-faced, disfigured, sweat-streaked creature.

"You get the fire ready," she said. "I'll be right back."

"Where are you going?"

"We must get something to put on your face. You will get sick if we don't do something about those bites."

"What...?" Before he could finish, she had run off to the woods away from the river. Miguel tiredly dropped his pouches and began gathering kindling and moss to start a fire. Once he had a fire going, he began gathering rushes and small feathered branches to spread their blankets on. He reclined on one of the blankets and before he knew it, had fallen fast asleep.

Oralia returned. Somewhere in her trip, she had stopped and scrubbed the mud from her face and legs and pulled the worst of the tangles out of her hair. After her initial shock at seeing her traveling companion horizontal, she smiled slightly with the realization that he was asleep. She contemplated him for a minute. *He is just a boy*, she thought, *a very tired and very dirty little boy*. She dropped her pouches next to the sleeping figure and, kneeling down, gently shook his shoulder.

"Miguel," she said. "Wake up." He was instantly awake, sitting bolt upright. A quick recognition of where he was came to him and he smiled sheepishly.

"I guess I fell asleep."

"You couldn't have been asleep too long. I haven't been gone that long, and the fire is going strong." Miguel leaned forward and threw a few more branches on the flames. Oralia opened her pouches and took out two bunches of plants.

"Here," she said, "I got some things to help your face."

She began shredding one of the plants and dropping it into a shallow bowl from her pouch. A strong astringent smell flowed from the bowl as she found a small rock and began crushing the shredded leaves. Miguel watched with interest as she took some water from a gourd and poured it into the bowl. Picking up the rock again, she continued to knead and crush the mixture. Finally, she took a band of cloth from around her neck. She dipped it in the mixture and leaned toward his face.

"I can do that," he said, reaching for the cloth.

"No, you can't. This must be rubbed on each of the bites. You cannot see where they are, although," she added with slight smile, "just about any place on your face is where they are. Let me get the ones on your face; you can do the ones on your arms when I am finished."

Miguel's resistance faded, and he leaned back while Oralia applied the solution to his face. She dabbed each bite and then scrubbed it vigorously. The solution stung slightly, and her scrubbing was not gentle.

"Close your eyes," she said softly as she worked up his face and around his eyes. "*Dios!*" she exclaimed, "you even have bites on your eyelids. Were you walking with your eyes closed?"

"You are not supposed to take the Lord's name in vain," was his answer.

"No," she replied without hesitation. "*You* are not supposed to take the Lord's name in vain. I am not a Christian. I can say whatever I want. You can open your eyes now." Miguel opened his eyes to see a pair of sparkling black eyes smiling at him.

"Here," she handed him the cloth, "do your arms. Scrub each bite to open it up a bit and let this get inside. It will help with the swelling and itching."

His face already felt slightly better. "What is it?" he asked.

Oralia shrugged. "A plant we have always used to treat small wounds. Father Juan said it is the same plant one of your warriors named Achilles used many years ago."

Miguel was a simple enlisted soldier in the Spanish army. He could read and write, but he had never heard of this hero Achilles. He would ask the corporal about him. As he rubbed his arms and hands, he periodically ran the rag back over his face. A decided coolness took hold. Oralia was busy with yet another shallow bowl and some liquid she poured from a small gourd she had with her.

"Do you think I need more of that?" he asked.

She looked up. "This is a different plant. This is the one I have been using all day. This one keeps the mosquitoes from landing on us. It is why you got bitten so badly today and I hardly at all. It is the medicine you refused to use this morning. We will both rub it on tonight before going to sleep. Everyone in the village uses this."

When the astringent had dried she handed the other bowl to him. "Put this on your hair, face, arms and hands. It will keep the mosquitoes away."

Miguel sniffed the bowl and recoiled as he had that morning. "It would keep *me* away, that is for sure. It smells awful. You will not be able to be near me."

Oralia smiled archly and replied, "Oh, it will not keep me away. You see," she rubbed the mixture through her hair and down her neck, "I will smell the same way. You will be too busy smelling yourself to notice me, and I will be too busy smelling myself to notice you."

"Miguel," she said, as they both finished applying the repellant substance, "I am too tired to eat. I am going to sleep now. I will eat well in the morning before we start out." She rolled herself up in her blanket and settled herself on the reeds that had been piled on one side of the fire. "*Buenas noches,* Miguel."

"*Buenas noches, Oralia...y gracias.*"

Wakefulness came slowly the next morning. The darkness behind her eyelids grew less, and then gray. Birds began fussing and chirping in the bushes nearby. Oralia opened her eyes and saw a gray, fog-shrouded dawn. As she lay there, struggling to full consciousness, she suddenly called out. "Miguel!"

He had been lying awake as well, and he answered. "Yes, what is it?"

"Do you smell it, Miguel?"

"What? That stuff I put on my face last night?"

Oralia sat up halfway. "No, silly." She took an exaggerated sniff. "Smoke; I smell smoke."

Miguel sat up and took a deep sniff. "Maybe; yes...yes, I smell smoke. What of it?"

Oralia gestured to their cold fire pit. "Our fire has been out for several hours. We are smelling smoke from a fire out there," she gestured to the east. "We are smelling Estella's fire!"

"Perhaps," he said. He jerked his head slightly upward. "With this fog, and no wind, smoke would stay close to the ground, but it could be some distance away. Still, you may be right. We should get going."

"Stay there for a minute," Oralia said. She got up and headed into the shrubbery. Realizing the task she was attending to, he lay back down and closed his eyes.

"Your turn," he heard, and opened his eyes to see Oralia building a fire. He got up and took his own trip into the shrubbery. Detouring on his way back, he walked down to the river. With luck and long stick, he managed to knock a duck senseless as it paddled in the shallows. He wrung its neck and took it back to the fire. He had it quickly plucked and disemboweled and on a spit over the fire. Oralia patiently held one of her small bowls beneath it and caught the dripping fat. She poured it over a mixture of roots and bread crumbs she was heating over the fire. As the duck cooked, Miguel cut off first the wings, and then slices from the breast, which they ate and washed down with water from the gourds they carried. As they were finishing, Miguel rose and said, "Let's get started."

"Just a minute," Oralia answered. She prodded and patted the remains of their meal into a few patties, heated them over the fire for a few minutes, and then after wrapping them in ferns, put two in her pouch and two in his.

"For lunch," she said. "For dinner, we will have something with Estella." They started off towards the east. As the day before, the trail of crushed and bent reeds was not hard to follow. It was late morning when they came across a ring of blackened stones. Miguel knelt down and felt the stones with his hand and then dug carefully down into the ashes.

"Still warm," He announced. "This is probably the fire you smelled this morning."

"It is Estella's fire," Oralia exclaimed excitedly.

Miguel felt compelled to correct her. "It is somebody's fire, and that somebody is heading east. We must be careful, though."

At Oralia's questioning look, he explained. "We think it is Estella, but we really don't know for sure. We must proceed cautiously. It could be a band of runaways from one of the missions, who will not be at all happy to see me. It could be a band of those war-like *Indios* from the valley, or *bandidos* who might be only too happy to see you." Again, Oralia fixed him with a questioning stare.

"You are a young woman, Oralia...attractive..." he managed to mumble. He let his sentence trail off.

"I see," she whispered.

"From here out, let me go in front," he suggested. "You stay a few *varas* back. Not so far that you cannot see me, but far enough where someone who sees me will not see you. If I signal like this," he pushed his hand in a downward motion "you must hide yourself in the reeds, and not get up until I come back for you. Understand?"

"Yes, I understand. Let's go."

They continued their march, although somewhat more slowly and decidedly more cautiously. Several hours of this travel brought them to late afternoon. Suddenly, Miguel crouched very low and gestured frantically with his right hand. Oralia threw herself down in the reeds and then instinctively rolled over several times to put herself away from the spot where she had dropped. She lay motionless for what she felt was an eternity. Finally, she heard someone coming through the reeds towards her. She hardly dared to breathe. The footsteps came closer and she could hear the person pushing and beating at the reeds. She shrunk down further. Finally, she heard a hoarse whisper.

"Oralia, Oralia, where are you?" With an immense sigh of relief, she rose to her knees. Miguel was only a few yards away, frantically searching the reeds.

"Miguel!" she gasped. He spun around and on seeing her a huge smile spread across his face.

"Ah, *ca...*," he checked himself. "Oralia, I thought I had lost you." The two young people approached and smiled warmly at each other.

"I think it is Estella!" he said excitedly. "I have only seen her once, when we went to the village to get Francisco for Father Danti's expedition." He added somewhat shamefacedly, "I did not pay that much attention to her. It is a young woman, but," he hesitated, "she is sitting on a large fallen log and she is crying, and...she does not have a baby with her." Oralia turned in the direction he had come from.

"Show me, show me where she is!"

They started back down the trail. In just a few minutes, Miguel stopped and put his arm out to stop Oralia.

"There," he pointed. Oralia followed his finger and saw from the back a dark head and a brightly colored shawl. She recognized the shawl.

"Estella!" she called. "Estella!" She ran forward. The seated woman jumped up and spun around. The log hid the entire lower half of her body, but even from this distance, Oralia could see a tear-streaked and confused face. Miguel stepped slightly back into the shrubbery. The two women threw their arms around each other and now both of them were sobbing convulsively.

Miguel stayed where he was. He would let Oralia tell him when it was wise to come forward. He saw the women talk excitedly together for a while, and then both of them disappeared behind the huge hump of the log. They stood, and in Oralia's arms was a wicker basket that she had her face buried in. Both women were smiling, now even laughing.

"I don't understand," said Estella. "What are you doing here? How did you find me?" Oralia gave the gurgling infant she was holding a final nuzzling and handed him back to his mother.

"I am here to help you find your husband's grave. I am here to bring you back to the village, and to the mission. I found you with the help of Father Juan and a very good young soldier." She turned back to where Miguel was hiding and motioned him forward. Estella began a step back and Oralia put a restraining hand on her arm.

"Stay here," she said firmly. "I have spent two days chasing you through this swamp, and you will stay here and listen to all I have to say and," she added looking in the direction of the young man walking towards them, "you will greet my friend with courtesy and graciousness."

"Your friend?" Estella began, but stopped abruptly as Miguel joined them.

"*Buenas dias, Señora*," he greeted her with a slight bow. He turned to the infant in his mother's arms. "This, I take it is Francisco's son. Is he Francisco as well?"

"He is," the mother answered somewhat coldly, taking a step back.

"And this," Oralia said, gesturing to the young soldier, "is my *friend*, Miguel." She continued brightly, "Now that everyone knows everyone, let us sit and talk about our plans."

She began the conversation. She told Estella that she, Father Juan, Castano, and Miguel had come to find her; and more importantly, to help her find her husband's grave. She told her that Miguel had been on the same expedition as Francisco, and that he knew where Francisco was buried and would take them to the site. She told her that they would help her to return his remains to Mission San Francisco. Finally, Oralia revealed that Estella was walking in the wrong direction, and that she would never find her husband's grave the way she was heading. At this last news, Estella began crying again.

"I did not realize how big the *pantanos* is. I have been wandering around for days, and have realized that I am on a hopeless search. That is why I was crying when you found me. I am so tired, I am hungry. If I go much longer without proper food, I will have no milk for my baby. I am so tired. I trusted to San Miguel to lead me to Francisco's grave. I am so tired." She dropped her head to Oralia's shoulder and sobbed.

Oralia patted her back and smoothed her hair and pulled her tightly to her. "Well, my dear friend, I don't think he is a saint," she smiled towards Miguel, "but I think this Miguel will lead you to your husband."

The group discussed among themselves the best course of action to pursue. Glancing around the site, they decided it provided all of the elements they needed to spend the night. Insisting that the exhausted Estella do nothing more than sit in the shade and rest with her baby, Oralia began preparing their campsite. Miguel went off to the river for water, and to see what he could find for dinner. When he returned with some mussels and three large frogs, the two women were delighted. Oralia prepared the dinner, insisting that Estella rest.

During dinner, Oralia gave Estella the further details of their little expedition. She explained that Father Juan and Castano were waiting for them not quite two days back. Once they were all together, they would begin the actual search for Francisco's grave. "I don't think it will take us more than a day to get there," Miguel offered. They all decided to get to bed early so that they could begin an early start back to where Father Juan and Castano were. "We cannot make it in one day," Miguel cautioned them, "but it will not take us two days. Maybe early afternoon of the second day."

Oralia had arranged sleeping pallets for her and Estella close together. Miguel's was on the other side of the fire. Before they settled down for the night, they all doused themselves, and the baby, with the foul-smelling repellent.

As they lay next to each other with the infant between them, Oralia reached over to her friend and gently stroked the side of her face and brushed her hair back. She began to ask her a question, but realized that the exhausted Estella was already sound asleep. Pulling the sleeping infant closer to her, she wished her friend a soft, "*Buenas noches, carita.*"

Morning came in the same stealthy way as it had the previous day. An awareness of light behind the eyelids, the twitter of birds, and the realization as Oralia opened her eyes that while it was still dark, the darkness was fading.

"*Buenas dias,*" she heard. Turning her head slightly, she saw her friend smiling fondly at her. "You are always there, when most I need you," Estella said.

The two friends decided it was still too dark to get up. Glancing across the smoking ruins of the fire, they saw Miguel, still huddled in his blanket, still sound asleep. They began whispering and giggling to each other.

"So," Estella began. "Tell me about this friend of yours." She threw her head in the direction of the sleeping soldier.

"What about him?"

"What about him! Is he a friend or a *friend*? You know what about him!"

Oralia remained deliberately vague. "He is a friend, *but* he could perhaps become a *friend*." She giggled and poked her friend. "It is good to see you concerning yourself with something other than wandering through the *pantanos*." She thrust the stirring infant lying between them to her friend. "Here, feed your son." She jumped up and hopped into the bushes.

Shortly after Miguel awoke, and after a quick breakfast, his usual map-making exercise, and a discussion of their plans for the day, they started off. He felt it necessary to make sure the two women knew of the plans.

"It will be very easy for us to find our way back because now we will be following the trail made by three people. Just remember," he added with a certain officiousness, "We will now be going the opposite way the reeds are bent." This was such an obvious fact to the two women that they could not resist glancing incredulously at each other, Oralia with an exaggerated rolling of her eyes.

¤ 24

Father Juan paced restlessly along the edge of their small campsite. It had been three days since Miguel and Oralia had left. *They should have been back by now. What could have happened to them?* He had thought they would be gone maybe two days, perhaps three, but not four. *Something must have gone wrong. They have run into hostile natives, or one of them has gotten sick or hurt. How long should I wait?* He had Miguel's map of how to get back to the mouth of the river, but there had been no discussion of how long they should wait before heading back there. *How long have we been gone from the mission? A week? Ten days?* He had lost all track of time. *I should have been keeping a log, or at least some device for marking the days off.*

He tried to think. *I know they left Castano and me three days ago. We crossed the bay and came up the river and spent the night on one day. It has only been four days. Not even a week. Only four days? I told Father de Landaeta we would be back in four days. We've been gone four days, and we haven't found Estella, and haven't found Francisco's grave. A year from now, will someone be trying to figure out what had gone wrong on my expedition? Father Danti lost one neophyte. It seems as if I may lose two neophytes, two gentiles, one soldier and myself. Madre de Dios!*

He walked back to the fire they kept burning all day. Castano had insisted that if they kept the fire burning the mosquitoes would stay away. Father Juan had to admit that it seemed to work, because other than when he wandered off into the woods, he did not get bitten. Even at night, when Castano heaped damp grasses on it to cause it to smoke more, mosquitoes did not seem to be such a problem.

Castano was working on what seemed to be a never-ending plaiting of grasses and reeds. Pausing in his pacing, Father Juan asked, as he had repeatedly for the past several days, "Where are they, Castano? What do you think has happened?"

The old man simply smiled and shrugged. "*Manana?*" he suggested. "Oralia knows the ways of the woods."

"I am sure Miguel knows 'the ways of the woods,' too," the priest answered shortly, "and you and I both know that the ways of the woods are unpredictable and dangerous. Where *are* they?"

Castano smiled, shrugged again, and turned his attention once more to stripping fibers from a pile of reeds he had at his feet. While Father Juan had spent the past several days worrying, pacing and praying, Castano had filled the hours with weaving and pounding and knotting. He had assembled a fair collection of lines, baskets and sharpened stakes, and he had put his implements to good use in keeping the two of them well fed. Father Juan pulled his watch out and consulted it. One o'clock.

He walked over to his lean-to and rummaged through his traveling pouch. It contained a rosary and his breviary, a tin cup and a few small planks that Castano had painstakingly shaved to narrow, concave platters. He took out the rosary and leaned back in the shade to begin the Sorrowful Mysteries. He felt almost guilty as he did, because he knew the rosary, especially on a warm drowsy afternoon, to be one of the most effective soporifics he had ever come across. Sure enough, halfway through the Carrying of the Cross, his words began to stumble, the beads fell from his fingers, and his head dropped down to his chest.

He was suddenly awakened by shouts and squeals. He looked up to see Castano standing and shouting towards the edge of the clearing. Miguel was approaching with a raised hand; following him was Oralia. Close behind was a smiling Estella, with her child slung in front of her!

"A feast! A feast!" Castano cried. "We will celebrate the return of our travelers." He headed back to several baskets he had buried at the edge of the woods. He had had four days of snaring, fishing, clubbing and gathering. He welcomed the famished travelers back with food much more substantial than anything they had been able to glean on their trek through the swamps. Father Juan and Estella visited while the others, no longer tired now that they were back with their companions, began preparing ducks, rabbits, and fish. There were still a few of the original corn cakes, now rock-hard, that they gleefully threw into a bubbling broth of rabbit and wild vegetables.

As they settled down to eat, Father Juan, Miguel and Estella blessed themselves and offered a prayer of thanks. Castano and Oralia respectfully bowed their heads. Oralia could not resist glancing up at Miguel. She had, in the past several days, seen him as competent woodsman and an excellent tracker, but perhaps most importantly, as a warm friend. She saw him now as devout young soldier offering obeisance to a God she did not understand.

After dinner, the group gathered around Miguel's maps and discussed the plans for the next day. Miguel pointed out again their position and the location of Francisco's grave.

"If we leave here early in the morning, we can be there by tomorrow afternoon. Then we can...," here he stumbled, "Um... do what we must do, spend the night, and be back at the mouth of the river by evening. We can build our signal fire for the boatmen, but they will decide when they can come across to get us. They will know when it is safe for them to come across. It may not be until the next morning, or even the next afternoon. I myself do not understand the tides and currents, but they seem to run twice a day, and the times and the directions change according to the seasons." He smiled,

"Perhaps we can enjoy a sunny day on the north side of the bay while we wait."

Oralia thought he cast a quick glance in her direction as he said this. Estella was to tell her later, "He *definitely* was talking to you when he said that."

Father Juan chimed in. "If we get to the mouth of the Rio San Joaquin tomorrow evening, we can be pretty sure that the earliest the boatmen will pick us up will be the next day. They will not try to cross the bay at night."

He cleared his throat. "Let me talk to you about what we must do when we find Francisco's grave." Oralia moved closer to Estella. "Francisco has been buried for almost a year now. As I understand it, he was wrapped in a blanket and buried somewhat shallowly. I want you all to understand what we will find in the grave. The soil where he is buried is damp, and at certain times of the year is under water. Given this, I expect the decomposition of Francisco's earthly remains to be largely completed." He looked quickly at Estella, but she was simply staring passively ahead. "There may be some parts of his clothing that remain, a belt or boots. There will be nothing that is recognizable of the Francisco you knew."

Miguel kept his silence, although it occurred to him that at the few burials of soldiers he had attended, the Spanish army had not been so foolish as to waste a perfectly good pair of boots. Father Juan continued. "Those of you who are Catholic should understand our belief."

Because he was not at all sure that *any* of them understood the church's teaching on death, resurrection, and a life hereafter, he elaborated. "We believe that humans are two parts, soul and body. The body is a temporary abode for the soul. A body dies. A soul never dies and lives forever. We believe that those who die in a state of grace have their *souls* immediately transported to heaven for eternal happiness with God. Their *bodies*, though, are subject to corruptibility and decay until the final judgment day. We believe that on that last day, all of the faithful will have their bodies resurrected to join their soul, and God, for all eternity. We will, at that final resurrection, have the most perfect bodies we have had on earth."

He looked up quickly around at the group. Oralia and Castano looked awestruck. The two faithful Catholics looked merely confused. Deciding that his impromptu theology class had gone woefully awry, he continued.

"I do not want anyone upset when we open the grave tomorrow. No one must be there except Miguel and me. We two will perform the work necessary." Although he tried to hide it, Miguel blanched and swallowed hard at the prospect. The priest continued. "We will place whatever remains there are in a suitable container for transport back to the mission. There, I will examine them carefully to see if there are any clues as to the cause of death, and when that is finished, we will re-bury Francisco in holy ground at San Francisco. Are there any questions?"

There were no questions, and only Estella had a comment. "I will be there, Father; I will be there when you open the grave."

25

The group came awake one by one the next morning. Castano was first and began building up the fire and heating some of the food left from the night before, along with some acorn mush. The others struggled from their sleeping shelters. Estella sat back against a pile of blankets and begin to nurse Francisco. Oralia brought her a bowl of the acorn gruel and a cup of water. Father Juan offered his morning prayers for a successful venture, and hopefully the end of this very trying journey. Miguel pored over his maps and climbed the tallest tree he could find. Finally, all had eaten, and leftover food was wrapped in ferns and stored away in pouches. Castano filled several of his baskets with water and poured them over the fire. He took a heavy stick and stirred the steaming ashes.

"Let's go," Miguel said. He gave a discreet wave of his hand to Oralia, and she moved up to join him at the head of the column. The others fell in behind them.

"Remember, Miguel," Father Juan could not resist calling. "Some of us are old, and some of us are more suited to a life of study, don't go so fast that we can't keep up."

The group marched for several hours before stopping for lunch. Now they did not stick to the high banks of the river, but crossed meandering waterways time and again. None of the streams were deep, but most of them had soft, muddy bottoms. Father Juan temporarily lost one sandal when he stepped ahead in the first stream they crossed. After that, he simply followed the examples of the natives, and tied his sandals around his neck before entering the water. Miguel was wearing boots fastened with some complicated arrangement of thongs and hooks, and he simply waded in with them on. He was constantly checking his map and consulting his compass. It did not miss anyone's attention that each time he scrutinized his map, Oralia was looking over his shoulder, making comments and pointing almost as much as he was.

At about two o'clock, he stopped the group and looked carefully around. They were on a slightly elevated piece of ground that sloped down to a broad meadow of grasses before it began rising again, to disappear first in reeds and then in a line of trees at the top of a low ridge. He told the group to wait there while he went forward a bit. Unbidden, Oralia, apparently now identifying more with Miguel than with the group, went ahead with him. He made no objection.

Miguel walked back and forth a few times, scrutinizing his map and taking readings from his compass. He would take a compass reading, put the compass down, pick up the map and make a notation. Now he called out words and numbers, and Oralia made entries on the chart. Father Juan could not help thinking to himself, *She is the assistant navigator!* With a twinge of regret, he recalled his many comrades who referred to the natives as "ignorant savages."

Miguel walked back to the group on the hill. "This is the place. This is where the battle was. I will have to look more carefully to find the grave, but I know this is the place. If you want to find a place to camp for the night, I will look for the grave."

"But Miguel," Estella asked, "didn't you mark the grave with a cross? Could you not just find the cross?"

Miguel gestured to the low-lying meadow. "*Señora*, we were here in early March. In late April and May, the snows from the Sierras," he gestured to the east, "begin flowing down the river. This would all be under water. The cross was probably washed away. I took very careful readings of the location of the grave. I will find it. Just give me time."

Father Juan and the others turned to erecting a camp site for the night. Estella tucked her infant to her breast and sat on the hillside, watching Miguel and Oralia crisscrossing the valley floor below her. Father Juan, as he helped with chores, kept glancing first to the east, where the figures of Miguel and Oralia stood out in the tall grass, and then to the west, where the sun was setting in the western sky. There was perhaps an hour of daylight left when they heard shouts from the meadow. Miguel and Oralia were standing together and gesturing. Estella was halfway to them before the rest of the group; as they ran up, the three figures were seen standing at the edge of a very slightly raised and fractured piece of ground.

"This is Francisco's grave," Miguel said.

"Are you sure?" Father Juan asked.

"I am sure," Miguel answered. "I took three bearings when we buried him: Two from the mountains to the south and the east, one from the grove of trees at the top of the hill. I had trouble finding it because in the past year, the grove of trees has changed slightly. The mountains, though, have not, and their bearings have given me an east-west orientation. I just had to find the north-south axis for that."

None of that meant anything to the assembled group, but there was no denying an oblong mound at their feet which, on closer examination, did not have the same growth pattern of weeds and grasses on it.

Looking up at the sky, Father Juan said, "It will soon be dark. Let us have our dinner and settle down for the night. We will finish this work in the morning."

Miguel and Oralia wandered off a bit and returned with several logs and branches. They placed them in a heap on the mound. "We will find the grave easily tomorrow," Miguel said.

The group turned and slowly walked back up the gentle slope. Oralia looked back and noticed that Estella was still standing at the site of the grave. "Go ahead," she said, to no one in particular. "I will be with you in a bit." She went back, put her arm around her friend's shoulder, and spoke softly to her. Finally, she gave her a kiss on the cheek, a final hug, and walked back to join the group on the hilltop. "Estella will stay at the grave for a while," she said.

26

Father Juan was the first one to wake the next morning. There were a few wisps of fog scattered here and there, and the sky overhead was the usual unrelenting gray. The air was damp and chilly. He stole softly over to the figure of the sleeping Miguel and gently shook him awake. Putting his fingers to his lips, he motioned to the young man to follow him. They walked a little way from the ring of sleeping figures to Father Juan's lean-to. Among the bundles lying beside the lean to were the two shovels. Handing one to Miguel, he picked up the other, along with a large wicker basket and a roll of canvas, and motioned to the young man.

"Let's go." They walked away from the campsite and down the hill. The fog lay more thickly in the small valley below, a lake of thick fog lying at their feet. None of the features of the land were visible. Father Juan paused and looked at Miguel.

"I know where it is," Miguel said, and led the way.

They walked slowly through the swirling mist. Nothing stood out until Miguel stopped and pointed to a looming shape ahead of them. Father Juan was surprised; he hadn't thought that Oralia and Miguel had piled the branches so high. With a gasp, he realized that it was Estella, half kneeling, sitting back on her heels. Her head and upper body were draped in a shawl. She turned at their approach, crossed herself and stood.

"*Buenas dias, Padre*; Miguel," she greeted them.

"*Buenas dias, Señora*. We are ready to bring Francisco's remains back to Mission Dolores."

Estella nodded slightly and took a few steps back. The two men set to work. The soil was soft and easily removed. When they had gone down several feet, they uncovered some few pieces of dirty gray material. "His blanket," Miguel whispered. Father Juan motioned to him to stop digging. He clambered up out of the shallow hole they had created and spread a piece of canvas on the ground at the edge of the grave. He looked meaningfully at the stolid woman standing there. Her expression changed not at all. He returned to the grave and told Miguel, "Dig very carefully and very shallowly. We should soon uncover the skeleton. When we do, stop digging and I will uncover it with my hands."

Miguel gave him a wide-eyed stare and nodded dumbly. Very shortly, a long brown bone was uncovered. Father Juan knelt and began clearing dirt away with his hand. He turned to Miguel. "Go get one of those baskets and wait at the edge with it." Miguel leaped out of the hole with an alacrity that startled the priest. While he was waiting, he looked again at Estella. She stood still at the graveside, staring down, her face devoid of any sort of emotion.

Miguel returned with the basket and, kneeling at the side of the grave, extended it toward the priest. Father Juan cleared more soil from around the bone and dropped it into the basket. He pronounced, primarily to himself, "Femur." He filled basket after basket with dirt, that Miguel dumped around the edges of the grave. It was a long and difficult process. Several times, Miguel glanced up the hillside and saw, in the dissipating fog, Oralia and Castano, standing and watching them.

After several hours of hand-digging, there was lying in the grave the clearly recognizable skeleton of a man, positioned on his back, his head turned to one side. Once more, Father Juan scrambled out of the grave. From one of his pouches, he took a plain stole that he draped around his neck, and a small vial of holy water. He stood beside Estella. He made the sign of the cross over the remains, sprinkled them with holy water, and intoned the familiar prayers, concluding, "*Requiescat in pace.*" He crossed himself, and his two silent companions did the same.

He turned to Estella. "My dear, I will now remove the remains to a container that we can carry back to the mission. I must tell you that as careful and as respectful as I will be, most of the tissue that holds the bones together is gone. I cannot assure you that when we get back to the mission the remains will be as you see them here." He was tempted to add, *In fact, when we get them back to the mission it will be just a jumbled pile of bones*, but he did not.

"I understand, Father. I have seen Francisco at rest where they buried him. I will be content to bring him back to San Francisco at all."

As the priest climbed back down into the grave, Estella gave one last glance at the skeleton, started to turn, but then turned back. She pointed to the rib cage. "There," she said quietly. The priest peered at the remains and saw what she was pointing out. A thin, black metal chain was entangled in the bones. He reached in and gently extracted the chain with a medallion attached.

"Francisco," Estella whispered.

The priest looked at the medal closely and rubbed some dirt from it. "You are right, my dear, it is Saint Francis."

"No," Estella said, reaching her hand out. "It is my Francisco." She explained, "It is a Saint Francis medal, one that I gave to my Francisco when we were married."

The priest dropped the medal and chain into her hand. She kissed it, and tightly closed her fist on it. "It is my Francisco, now I know for sure." She turned and walked slowly up the hill.

Father Juan told Miguel to go up the hill and get one of the larger reed baskets that Castano had made. When he brought it back, the priest began to carefully lift the bones and place them in the basket. Miguel stood by uneasily; he could not bring himself to handle the yellowing material.

Father Juan started at the feet. The basket was only large enough to hold the bones if they were piled on top of each other. He reasoned that the skull on top made the most sense. Working under this method, he had reached the upper torso when he suddenly stopped, staring at the piece of flat bone he had in his hand. He looked back down in the grave where the bone had lain. Small fragments of bone covered the scant traces of gray blanket mingled with the soil. He stared again at the broad, flat bone in his hand. *Madre de Dios,*" he whispered.

27

Since it had taken longer than anticipated for Father Juan to properly remove the remains from the grave, there was no disagreement when the decision was made to spend one more night on the hillside, and to begin an aggressive trek to the river's mouth early the next morning. Father Juan took the basket with the remains and left it at the edge of his lean-to. It was a quiet and subdued group that sat down to the evening meal, and all of them retired to their sleeping mats almost as soon as the sun set.

Father Juan lay on his mat and thought over and over again of the remains lying just outside of his crude shelter. There was no doubt from Miguel's precise map, from the grey blanket pieces, and most of all from the St. Francis medal that Estella had so readily recognized, that the body they had unearthed was Francisco's. There was also no doubt, from the shattered scapula that he had examined, that Francisco had been shot.

Estella's unaccountable insistence that her husband had not gotten sick and died had been accurate. He had proof positive of that, and he was convinced that when he was able to examine the remains more carefully, he would find further proof. But what did he do with this information? Who did he share it with? His superior? Certainly. The army? Yes. Estella? *God help me,* he prayed once again. As she had clutched the Saint Francis medal and turned from the grave, he had noted a calmness on her face that he had never seen before. She was accepting and resigned, and at peace. Now was he going to drag her back into a tormented world of questions without answers and anger with no outlet? *There are answers, though,* he thought. *They are hidden, but they are there. I have helped her find her husband, and now I must help her find the answers. God help me.* It was no startled exclamation. It was a sincere and fervent cry for help.

When the group started back the next morning, Father Juan was convinced he had just spent another entire night without sleeping. How many nights could one go without sleeping before falling asleep, no matter what you were doing, in the middle of the day? He had tossed and turned enough nights on this miserable expedition to know that there were periods of sleep, perhaps several hours stitched together here and there. But he never woke in the morning refreshed and ready for the day. Today was no different. After a quick and subdued breakfast, Miguel began leading the group back. Father Juan followed him with Estella slightly behind him. Oralia and Castano came next, the basket holding "their brother" swinging slightly between them as they walked side by side. Perhaps because they were all finally heading home and looking forward to putting this grim episode behind them, the conversation was a little more animated this morning. There was nothing lighthearted or frivolous about it, but comments were made about the rising sun, the prospects for a fair day and how long it might take them to reach the mouth of the river.

All but Miguel seemed pleasantly surprised when, well before noon, he stopped the party and, pointing to an ever-widening estuary to the west, told them they were there. They immediately began gathering all the driftwood and dried timber they could find, and started a large, smoky fire on one of the beaches. After that, there was nothing to do but sit and wait.

Late that afternoon, two canoes appeared on the horizon and quickly made their way to the beacon still burning on the beach. It was not the same two who had taken them across. They seemed somewhat dismayed to find two extra passengers awaiting them. They could start back now; it would be light for several more hours, the tides were favorable and their companions at Yerba Buena would light their own fire to guide them if darkness came before they were back. They were unsure, though, about the extra passengers and the safety of the canoes.

After much discussion and consideration of the weather, it was decided that if the bundles and parcels were left behind, and there was some judicious distribution of passengers by weight, they could make it. Father Juan decided that since they all planned to sleep in their own abodes this evening, the shovels, canvases, blankets and mats could be left behind. The only parcel they *had* to take was the basket with Francisco's remains. Even with those arrangements, however, when the two oarsmen got ready to step in their canoes, they shook their heads. "No, too heavy." They pointed to the very narrow space between the water and the top of the canoe's side. Miguel suddenly jumped ashore. "I will stay one more night. You go back and send another canoe for me tomorrow."

"Are you sure?" Father Juan looked doubtful.

"Of course," the young man smiled. "Do you think I am in a big hurry to get back to drilling and marching at the *presidio*? Tell the corporal that he will have to get along without me for one more day." He pointed to the abandoned parcels and blankets strewn about the beach. He smiled broadly. "I will have a very comfortable camp site tonight, and the weather is fair."

Reassured, Father Juan allowed the canoes to push off. They had barely begun drifting, however, when suddenly, "I will stay too," Oralia declared, and before anyone could stop her, she jumped into the waist-deep water. The canoes were now well out in mid-stream and beginning to drift down river.

Father Juan sat dumbfounded, but Estella smiled and waved to her friend, who gave her a wide grin back. Miguel waded out to take her hand and help her to shore.

The trip across the bay was swift and smooth. Once into the bay, the canoes this time were pointed towards the inland side of the bay. They paddled past a wide expanse of mud flats and then across, to have some hidden current carry them along the western shore and back to Yerba Buena just as the sun was setting. Father Juan could see a tall, gray-robed figure on the small pier, and he knew Father de Landaeta had come down to greet him.

"Juan, Juan, *bienviendo*! I am so glad to see you." He gave the younger priest a warm embrace. He stepped back and held him at arm's length. "How are you, *hijo*? We worried about you. You took longer than we thought. Was your trip a success?" He looked around at the disembarking passengers. "Ah, Estella!" he exclaimed joyfully, embraced her and then frowned. "Where is Private Galindo?"

Father Juan smiled tiredly and reassured the superior. "All is well, Father. The private is well. Because we were bringing Estella and her child with us, we could not fit all in the canoes. Private Galindo," he found the phrase awkward after a week of "Miguel," "volunteered to wait another night at the river's mouth. We will send a canoe for him tomorrow. It was very noble of him."

"I hope he will be all right," Father de Landaeta said.

"I am sure he will be just fine," a smiling Estella said. Father Juan decided not to elaborate, and Father de Landaeta had apparently not noticed the absence of Oralia.

Father Juan gestured towards the basket now lying on the pier. "We have brought Francisco back, Father, for burial in holy ground." The superior bowed his head and made the sign of the cross over the container. Estella turned to leave with Castano at her side.

"I am going back to the village, Father," she said. "Thank you for your concern for me, and for sending Father Juan after me. I think I will not be at the mission for work tomorrow, but I will be there the next day. When will we bury Francisco?"

"Well, tomorr..." the superior began. Father Juan interrupted.

"Father, it has been a very tiring and very difficult trip for all of us. Perhaps we could, as Estella suggested, take tomorrow as a day of rest, and plan to bury Francisco the next day. I am sorry, Father; I have lost all track of time. What is tomorrow?"

"Why, it is Tuesday."

"Could we perhaps then plan to bury Francisco on Wednesday?" He looked to Estella. She nodded her head.

"*Si*, Wednesday would be a good day. Good night, Fathers."

Father de Landaeta gestured to two of the neophytes who had accompanied him to pick up the basket, and they began the walk back to the mission. As they walked down one of the narrow streets, Father de Landaeta pointed to the sign on a low building fronting a large lot with blocks of stone strewn about. "Xavier Ibarra, Stonemason," it read. The priest stood in wonderment while his superior clapped him on the shoulder.

"It seems as if your friend had found what he considers a suitable surname."

Father Juan could only stare in bemusement. He had found, in his calling to the priesthood, a wonderfully fulfilling vocation. His parents had been approving and proud. Still, when he announced his plans to be ordained, his father had felt compelled to pull him aside one evening. "It is a wonderful calling, Juan, and we are blessed that you have chosen it; but remember, *hijo*, that as a priest, you will have no son to carry on your name." At the time, that had not really been a consideration, and he had since not given it much thought. Now, though, he could only shake his head in slight regret, that his father would never see that sign nor know the story behind it.

As they approached the mission, torches were just being lit on some of the walls, and from the windows the soft glow of lanterns shone. Father Juan directed the two neophytes to place the basket in his room, and paused to say goodnight to his superior.

"Father," he added, "I would like to visit with you tomorrow. Perhaps right after lunch? I'd like to give you a full report on the expedition."

"That would be good, Juan. I am very interested in hearing of your expedition. I could actually see you in the morning."

Father Juan considered carefully. "No; there are a few things I would like to take care of in the morning. Right after lunch would be better."

"Good. Come to my office after lunch," the superior said, "and we will visit on several things. I do want to tell you that my letter of request for reassignment has been received by the father president and is being considered."

"That is good, Father. I know that is what you want. For now, I need to get a good night's sleep on a real bed. *Buenas noches.*"

28

He was awakened the next morning by the bells calling the monks and the faithful to Lauds. He smiled pleasantly when he realized that he had slept all night. No twigs or rocks digging into his hips, no mosquitoes buzzing around his head, no rustlings or animal calls from the bushes. He rose and looked back at his narrow cot—a cowhide stretched tight on a wooden frame and covered with coarse woolen blankets. It had been as comfortable and comforting to him as a plush, velvet-covered mattress reserved for a king.

At the morning service, his thoughts were called back to the mornings of the past several days. They had been mornings of discomfort and worry, but they had been mornings with the wonders of God's world all around him. Regretfully he admitted to himself that his morning prayers then had been hurried and uncomfortable. As he listened the canticles now, in the warm comfort of the chapel, he heard the familiar prayers with a new appreciation that he realized he had acquired in the *Pantanos*:

> *Bless the Lord, all waters above the heavens*
> *Bless the Lord, all rain and dew*
> *Bless the Lord, every wind*
> *Bless the Lord, seas and rivers*
> *Praise the Lord, from the earth, sea creatures and all oceans*
> *All mountains and hills, beasts, wild and tame, reptiles and birds on the wing.*

Lauds is a prayer of praise, primarily for the wonders of nature, and he realized that only when one had wrested with those wonders firsthand could one realize the true significance of those ancient prayers.

As he walked across the courtyard to the refectory, he noticed that the sky was clear, and even at this early hour, the day was warm. *Well*, he thought to himself, *it is September. I suppose after one of the coldest summers I have ever experienced, I shouldn't be surprised to find a warm autumn.*

Breakfast was another almost-new experience after his sojourn in the wild. He sat at a table and had hot food on clean dishes brought to him. He didn't have to try and balance some rock-hard bread and unidentifiable gruel on a wooden plank on his lap, while he ate with his fingers. He silently composed his own canticle of praise:

He realized he was probably being sacrilegious and left off his irreverent prayer. He was pulled fully back from his reveries by a voice at his side.

"How was your trip to the *Pantanos?*" Father Danti sat down on the bench across from him.

"Good, good," he replied noncommittally.

"Did you find our wandering neophyte?"

"Yes, in fact we did."

"More importantly, did you convince her to return to the mission and her duties?"

"Yes, we did. Actually, though, the father superior has granted her some time off, before she returns to the looms." Although this was a slight exaggeration, it was true that the father superior had acknowledged that she would not be at work today.

Father Danti gave a snort of disgust. "Typical! One of the neophytes breaks all the rules of the mission and runs away and when she returns, he rewards her with a holiday. And then," he continued, "he wants to know why I have a problem with discipline."

"Jesus told us the story of the Prodigal Son. In this case, it is a prodigal daughter who is welcomed with open arms," Father Ibarra could not resist throwing out.

"And her late husband?" Father Danti continued. "Was there any trace of him?"

Father Juan considered very carefully what he wanted to disclose at this point. He finally offered, "A trace is a good term, Antonio. We did uncover his remains. In fact, they are right now reposing in my cell. Except for the skull, they would, to the average person, be hardly recognizable as human remains. A pile of bones is probably how I would characterize them. I must admit that you and your party gave him a very adequate burial."

Father Danti seemed to have exhausted his desire for conversation, and stood to leave.

"I told you we had buried him; why did you want to bring the remains back here?"

"Francisco was a member of our faith, Antonio, as is his wife. She wanted him interred in holy ground and that is what we will do. Tomorrow, in fact, if you want to attend the service."

"I'll see what is on my schedule," Father Danti blurted, and walked away.

Father Juan did not tarry after breakfast but hurried to his cell. He called to two Indians and asked them to bring one of the smaller tables from the dining room to his cell. When they had wrestled it through the door, it barely fit into the small space, and that only after they had taken his writing desk and chair out. Dismissing the neophytes, he closed the door to his cell and dragged the basket of bones out and sat it on the floor next to the table. Taking a deep breath, he took a blank journal, laid it on his bed and began reassembling the skeleton on the table. It didn't take him long before a clearly recognizable human form—feet, legs, pelvis; rib cage, arms, hands and head—lay supine on the table. Many of the smaller extensions, vertebrae and more deeply-placed bones, he had to lay to the side in their approximate location. His last anatomy class had been many years ago, but he couldn't suppress a slight smile. His professor would have been pleased with him.

He began a very careful examination of the bones of the upper torso, with the scapula that had caught his attention the other day. He made some notes in the journal, placed the scapula where it belonged, and crouched down at the head of the table. He made more notes, examined some of the rib bones, made more notations, and returned to the scapula. He looked at the clavicles and tried to place them in a correct relation to the other bones of the upper torso. Finally, he left his examination of the bones in order to make extensive notes, and when he was finished with those, he stood back with a sigh of satisfaction. It was almost lunch time, so he left his cell. Probably for the first time since he had occupied it he locked the door. As he stepped out to the patio, he was struck with a blast of hot air. It was a hot in San Francisco! Not sunny, not warm—truly hot. He guessed the temperature to be at least forty degrees. As he walked across the courtyard, the heat was reflected off the walls of the surrounding buildings. Even in all his time in San Diego he had never felt weather this hot. He looked around to see if there was a fire raging somewhere near. No smoke and no fire were anywhere in evidence.

The weather was the talk of the dining room. A few of those who had been in San Francisco for a while dismissed it, saying, "We get a few days like this every autumn. It will last two or three days and then return to normal." Father Juan, after four months of fog, cold, and a few brief periods of sunshine, tentatively asked, "What *is* normal in San Francisco?"

"Fog," was the immediate answer from several quarters.

As they finished up their lunch, Father Juan approached Father de Landaeta. "Father," he asked, "can you come and visit with me in my cell?"

"Yes, Juan, now is a good time. Let's go."

The two priests stepped out into the blazing sunshine and hurried across the courtyard. They stepped into the shaded corridor running down the side of the building. Father Juan took the key from his robe and ushered the perplexed superior into the coolness of the small room. Father de Landaeta stepped into the tiny room and stopped abruptly at the scene that confronted him: the table filling almost the entire room, and on it, the grinning visage of Francisco's skeleton.

"Juan!" the superior gasped, stepping back. "What are you doing? This is diabolical." He crossed himself and tried to back out the door. Father Juan stopped him with gentle hands on his shoulder.

"No, Father, no; I am doing only my work as a physician. I am only doing my work in studying the deaths of the neophytes at Mission Dolores. I have uncovered an interesting cause of death of our poor Francisco." He looked intently at the other priest. "If you would prefer, we can discuss it somewhere else, but there are things I need to show you."

Father de Landaeta sighed and shook his head. "No, I am fine. I was just startled when I first saw this." He gestured towards the skeleton. "I am fine now. Let us discuss this 'interesting cause of death' you mention."

Father Juan closed the door behind them, and the two priests edged past the table and sat on the bed. Father Juan picked up his journal, put it in his lap and began.

"Father de Landaeta, this," he gestured towards the table, "is the earthly remains of Francisco, the neophyte who died on the expedition last year. We know that because his burial site had been carefully plotted by Private Galindo and we used that map to locate the grave. We also know that this is Francisco because his widow was there when I unearthed these remains, and she was able to identify a small item of personal adornment that she had given to him when they were married and that he always wore—a Saint Francis medal."

"Yes, Juan," the somewhat wary superior replied, "we accept that this is Francisco."

"Unfortunately, Father," the younger priest continued, "you must also accept that Francisco did not die of disease as we have been told. It is obvious from a careful examination of his remains that he was shot."

Father de Landaeta's eyes widened, and he responded almost immediately. "This is very serious, what you are saying, Juan. You are saying not only that we have been lied to about the cause of this young man's death; you are also accusing someone of causing his death by violence. By murder!"

Father Juan stood up slowly and placed his journal back on the cot. "Let me give you my reasons for making what I know is a most serious allegation." He stepped over to the table and retrieved two flat pieces of bone, each about the size of his hand.

"These are the scapula, or what we call the shoulder, or wing bones." He reached around the other priest and pressed the back of his shoulder. "If you were an angel, Father, your wings would be attached here." He held up the bone in his right hand. "This is the right scapula bone of Francisco." He held up his left hand. "And this is the left scapula bone of Francisco; notice the difference." The left bone was much smaller than the right and its edges, instead of being smooth and curving, were jagged and irregular. "This bone has been shattered, as can only be done by a high-speed projectile—a bullet."

The other priest interrupted him. "What about a sword, or a spear? That is a very thin bone."

Father Juan answered, "A sword or a spear could indeed penetrate this bone, but it would not shatter it, it would crack it. This bone is pulverized. I have some of the larger chips on the table, but much of it is missing. The missing pieces are powder and chips still resting in the grave." He put the two pieces of bone down and returned to the skeleton, and picked up two of the rib bones, one of them displaying the same jagged end as the scapular and the other, a small, rounded chip. "These are his second and third ribs from the left side." He placed them on the table and picked up two more. "These are the same ribs, from the right side. You can see that the ones on the left are damaged, undoubtedly by the same bullet. A musket at close range is a very powerful weapon, Father. A bullet went through Francisco's back, through his scapular bone—probably through his lungs—hit two of his ribs, and finally exited through his chest. Death would have been almost instantaneous."

"You should also know," he added, "I can tell, from the angle of the bullet's path, that Francisco was shot by someone standing a little higher than he was, and we know from Private Galindo's sketch of the battlefield that the soldiers were in fact higher on a slope than the neophytes. Also, we know, of course, that the soldiers were the only people who had firearms. There is no suggestion that any of the fleeing runaways had firearms." He concluded, "Francisco was killed, probably by accident, by one of the soldiers, and they have tried to cover that up." He replaced the pieces of bone he had been using to exhibit his theory and stood facing his superior.

Father de Landaeta was slumped over, with his arms on his knees, his hands clasped in front of him. He could have been in prayer. Finally, he looked up. Father Juan had never seen the older man so drawn and haggard.

"This is terrible Juan. This is awful. I don't know what to do. I must think about this. Poor Estella; some soldier...the poor soldier...poor Francisco! Juan, I must think about this. Please, I abjure you, do not tell anyone of this, not yet. I promise you, we will not keep something like this secret. We will tell the truth, but I must think about this." He rose unsteadily and began shuffling towards the door. "I must pray. Please come to my study after evening prayer. Please?" he finished plaintively.

Father Juan put a hand on the old man's arm. "Of course. Until this evening, Father. I am sorry."

He opened the door for the older priest. The outside air blew into the thick-walled adobe room like a blast from a furnace. *Like a blast from hell*, Father Juan thought. *This place has become a taste of hell. Well,* he reconsidered, *at least purgatory.*

29

At the evening meal, again the talk was of nothing but the weather. "It won't last long," was the consensus. As far as Father Juan was concerned, it couldn't last long enough. After months of mostly fog, interspersed with at best weak sunlight, he found the change invigorating. When he mentioned that, one of the brothers gently remonstrated him.

"That is fine for us to say. We enjoy the shade and coolness of adobe buildings. I assure you, the *Indios* working in the fields or putting up more of those adobe buildings do not find it so pleasant."

"You are right," an abashed Father Juan admitted. He turned towards the father superior. "Do you think, Father, we should consider adjusting the worker's hours while the weather is so hot? They are not used to it and must be suffering."

"I hadn't considered that," the superior answered vaguely.

"We are not in a position to reduce our output," Father Danti said. "The army is in great need of both our produce and our woolen products and," he added, "they pay us well for them." He stared significantly at Father de Landaeta. Still the superior made no attempt to elaborate on his last comment.

Father Juan addressed Father Danti. "I wasn't suggesting reducing our output. Perhaps though, an adjustment in hours? More time off in the heat of the day, or beginning work earlier in the day? Or working in the evening hours when it is cooler."

"This heat will last only two or three days; it will be too much effort to adjust the schedules and then return them to normal in just a few days," was Father Danti's final objection.

"Juan, visit with me in my office." The superior rose to leave. He turned to Father Danti. "Father Antonio, the neophytes' work schedule is entirely up to you." He strode from the dining room. As Father Juan prepared to follow him, he couldn't help but notice the smug smile on Father Danti's face.

The sun had set, and while the courtyard air was still warm, there was no blast of heat as he stepped outside. He walked across to the superior's office. The door was half open and with a perfunctory knock, he walked in. A weary-looking Father de Landaeta sat behind his desk. He waved a hand to one of the chairs. There was no offer of chocolate, or brandy. There was no desultory small talk.

"What do we do, Juan?" Father de Landaeta asked. Although Father Juan was fairly certain his superior had an answer to the question, he answered readily.

"I must report my findings to the authorities."

Father de Landaeta nodded and corrected him. "*We* must report your findings to the authorities. We will go tomorrow, you and I, and tell Colonel Alberni what you have discovered. We must do that before we bury Francisco. They may want to see the proof of your conclusion."

"I hadn't thought of that, Father," Father Juan said. "That actually brings up something else we must do besides report my findings to the colonel." At the superior's questioning look he continued. "We must tell Estella what really happened to her husband. She has never accepted that he died of disease, and now that we know that he didn't, we cannot keep it from her."

"How do you think it is best to manage that?" the beleaguered superior asked.

"If you wish, Father, I will tell her. We have established a certain rapport, she and I, and I think my help in finding her husband has only strengthened it. I will talk with her before we go to the *presidio*." He paused for a minute and then suggested, "This may be an opportune time for me to mention something else. I wonder if you could change Estella's assignment from the looms?"

"Why do we want to do that?" Father de Landaeta asked.

"Estella, with her insistence on finding her husband, has seriously antagonized Father Danti. I am not sure if it has occurred to you, Father, but Father Danti is at least complicit in the false report that Corporal Montoya filed."

It was obvious that such had *not* occurred to the superior, because he brought both hands up to his face and rubbed it wearily. "No, it had not," he confirmed.

Father Juan explained. "Father Danti never tried to contradict the corporal's report, although he must have known it was false. In fact, he has repeatedly asserted that Francisco died of an illness. He had to have known that was not true. Apparently, his close relationship with the soldiers overrode his good judgment. He did not want any of them disciplined for the shooting of Francisco. Now, because of Estella's insistence, both the corporal and Father Danti are going to be found out to be involved in a serious lie. Having Estella working directly under Father Danti, at the looms, would be asking for his anger, and her further unhappiness."

"I understand what you are saying, Juan, but all of the neophytes work under Father Danti. How can we employ her without having her report to him?"

"I have not had an assistant for my work since Guillermo was sent to Monterey. Estella is a very bright and industrious lady. She would make a very good assistant for me. In fact, once I return to Monterey, she would probably be very competent at providing medical care to the neophytes. This mission, I think more than any other, should have a clinic on site to care for the persistent illnesses that plague it. I think she would be very good at that. Assign Estella to be my assistant."

Father de Landaeta considered all of this very carefully and finally agreed. "I will tell Father Danti this evening that tomorrow, when she reports for work, Estella is to be sent to you. I will tell him that I have decided that she is to be your new assistant. I will leave it to you, Juan, to give her your findings. You must do that as soon as she reports to you tomorrow. Once you have done that, you and I will want to visit Colonel Alberni. We cannot let this wait any longer. Please, as soon as you have spoken with Estella, come to my office and we will go to the *presidio*."

"That is a sensible plan," Father Juan answered. "I don't know how she will receive the unfortunate news I have to give her. All of my experience with Estella suggests it will not be any way that I might anticipate, but there is nothing to be done for it. I will talk with her tomorrow."

"Good, good," Father de Landaeta said. "This is a very sensitive matter and must be handled sensitively. Let me be sure we are in agreement on this. First, you will tell Estella what you have discovered. Next, you and I will tell Colonel Alberni what you have discovered. Then Alberni will have to decide what the next steps are. Agreed?"

"Yes, I think that is correct, Father; that will be the way we handle it."

"Good, good. *Buenas noches*, Juan." The superior rose, then added, "He is Italian, you know." At Father Juan's perplexed look, the superior went on absently, "Alberni, Colonel Alberni; he was an Italian soldier who got tired of their internecine wars and offered his services to King Carlos."

"Uh, yes; I see," answered a thoroughly confused Father Juan, although he didn't.

¤ 30

The first thing Father Juan had done after his meeting with Father de Landaeta had been to return Francisco's bones to the cramped confines of the basket they had used to bring him to the mission. This he had placed under his cot.

Now, he awaited the arrival of Estella. The day had dawned as clear and warm as the previous two, and he wondered if all the speculation about this hot weather being an anomaly was correct. Perhaps this was just the normal beginning of San Francisco's summer, and it would be this way until winter, which he mused would be some other bizarre manifestation from the norm.

A slight knock on the open door of his office announced Estella's arrival. She stood in the doorway with her child slung in a pouch in front of her. It occurred to Father Juan that he had never seen Estella without the child. As he thought about it, he realized that a child not yet weaned would have to always be with the mother, whether she was at prayer or work or in her own hut.

"Father Danti said you wanted to see me, Father," she announced.

"Yes, yes, dear. Please come in." He gestured to a chair. "Please have a seat. Did Father Danti tell you what it was about?"

"No," she answered with a slight smile. "He just said, 'Never mind starting at your loom. Your *friend*, Father Ibarra, wants to see you.'"

"I am sorry, my dear, if Father Danti made it sound unpleasant."

Her smile widened slightly. "Father Danti makes everything sound unpleasant."

The priest put his head back for a moment, composed himself, and began. "There are two things I want to discuss with you, Estella. One I hope will be easy and pleasant. The other might be a little more difficult."

"Well, Father, let's begin with the easy one."

"Father de Landaeta has assigned you to be my assistant. You will no longer be working at the looms." Estella said nothing and maintained the same expression on her face. Father Juan continued. "I have need of an assistant. I would like to begin training you in the skills necessary for taking care of the neophytes who are ill. We are planning on opening a little infirmary here at the mission. We will need someone to help take care of those who are sick. I think you could be very good at that. I need someone who can eventually handle such duties on their own. Sometime, probably not too long from now, I will be sent back to *San Miguel*. Before then, I would like to begin teaching you the things you will need to bring some comfort to your people. Would you like to do that?"

Estella now smiled openly and said, "I would, Father. I think I would like that very much. Thank you for giving me this opportunity."

"Good, good," the priest answered. "We will begin today. Each day now, instead of going to the looms you will come here, and I will teach you all you need. Now..." his voice trailed off, "now, as to the other matter I mentioned."

"Yes, Father," she leaned slightly forward.

"I have examined Francisco's remains in great detail. I have more information to offer you about his death." Now she sat completely on the edge of her chair. "I am afraid, my dear, that your suspicions about your husband's death were correct." Her face was an intense demand to proceed, and to proceed immediately. "I have examined Francisco's remains very carefully and I am quite sure that Francisco died from a gunshot wound." Estella gave a sharp exhalation of breath and leaned back in the chair. Father Juan, prepared to catch a slumping figure, watched her warily.

"Lies. I knew it," she whispered.

"You are right, my dear; we have all been lied to."

"Why?" she asked. "Why would they kill Francisco? What could he have done? Francisco was not bad. He obeyed all the orders of the priests and the soldiers. Why would they shoot him?" She suddenly jumped up from the chair and leaned over the desk. "They have murdered him! They cannot do this! I want them arrested. Who did this? The soldiers, the soldiers cannot just shoot people when they feel like it. They must be punished." She collapsed back in the chair and began sobbing.

Father Juan began gently. "In fact, my dear, Father de Landaeta and I are going to the *presidio* this morning to report this. We will report to the colonel himself. We will tell him that we demand that the soldier who did this must be punished. You must understand, my dear, that I think Francisco's death was an accident. I think he was shot by mistake. Nonetheless, it should be punished, and they should not have lied about it. We will make this clear to the colonel."

Estella's sobs lessened. She shook her head slowly. "I knew it," she repeated. "I just knew that Francisco had not died of an illness."

"Estella," the priest continued, "I know this is awful news to you. You have been terribly treated in this matter, and I know that you are hurt and angry. I must, though, ask of you a favor." She looked at him in bewilderment. "As I said, Father de Landaeta and I are going this morning to report this matter to Colonel Alberni. We will demand that the soldiers responsible be punished. Although no amount of money will ever make up for the loss of Francisco, we will demand that the Spanish army, which is responsible for your husband's death, pay you a just sum for the harm they have done you...'

"I don't want their money!" she spat.

"I understand," the priest said. "Nevertheless, whatever is done, I must ask you to not mention this to anyone until we have had a chance to talk to the colonel. As upsetting as this news is to you, it will also be upsetting to all the other neophytes. We must give the colonel an opportunity to show the people that he will not let this act go unpunished. Once we have discussed this with the colonel you will be free to tell anyone you wish, but please give us the opportunity to report it first."

Estella sat unmoving in the chair. "I knew. I *always* knew. I don't care who else knows. You have done me a great service with this. As you request, I will not say anything to anyone about it. I do not need to. Once you tell the colonel of it, it will be all over the *presidio*, the town, the village and the mission. What I want to know is, will there be anything but talk? Someone must be punished. My husband was murdered."

Father Juan decided not to engage her any further in parsing the words used to describe her husband's death. "God bless you, my dear," he said softly, "we will go and report this now. Please stay here, in my office, while I am gone. This is your new workstation. Familiarize yourself with my books and journals, and when I return, I will begin explaining them to you." He left her still processing this news, and went to find the father superior.

As they walked down to the *presidio*, the two priests discussed how they would handle their meeting. It was decided that Father Ibarra would detail to the colonel his findings, offering him proof if needed, and Father de Landaeta would claim the authority of his office in demanding that justice be done.

When they were seated in the colonel's office and the preliminary courtesies had been disposed of, Father de Landaeta began the conversation by telling the colonel that they were here to discuss a matter of "very grave concern," and that it concerned the "behavior of his troops." The colonel motioned to the priests to wait just a moment and went to the door and stuck his head out.

"Sergeant!" he called.

"Sir." Sergeant Amador answered, and was immediately at the door.

"I think you had better come in and listen to what the fathers have to say."

When the sergeant was seated, Father Ibarra began. He told them that it concerned the expedition led by Father Danti and Corporal Montoya last March. He told them that, as they knew, ever since the expedition and the death of Francisco, there had been stories and mumblings that something had gone wrong on that expedition. He told them how, after his study of all the events and all the stories, he had discounted and finally dismissed those stories. He went on to explain how and why he had decided to accompany the widow of the dead man in her efforts to recover his body. He gave a quick synopsis of that trip and of their ultimate discovery of the grave. He made it a point to mention that it was due in large part to the excellent mapmaking skills of Private Galindo, and to the leadership abilities the private had displayed on that trip, that they had had any success at all. The sergeant made a quick note. Finally, the priest described to them what he had discovered when he examined the remains carefully.

At this news both the colonel and the sergeant interrupted him. "Are you sure of what you are saying?" the colonel asked. "Have you seen this type of wound before?" And, "Have you treated men who have been shot?" the sergeant asked.

"I am sure of what I am saying. If you wish, I can show you the remains. Neither of you would dispute what I am saying if you saw the shattered bone. Yes, I have treated men who have been shot, but no, I have never seen this type of wound. I have only read descriptions of it and seen illustrations in textbooks." He went on. "May I ask you gentlemen? Have you seen this type of wound before? Have you seen men whose bones have been struck by a musket ball?" Both men nodded silently. He continued, "Tell me, think about it and tell me what it was you saw."

After a moment of pensive silence, the sergeant began. "A musket ball traveling through flesh is really not too bad. But when that ball hits bone, it is the bone and not the ball that causes most of the damage. You have told us of a 'shattered bone;' a shattered bone is a good description. A bone hit by a musket ball becomes itself a damaging instrument. The bone becomes a hundred balls, each one spreading out and causing damage. What you have described is what happens."

"I still have the bones which you can examine," Father Juan suggested.

The colonel thought for a minute about this and finally addressed the sergeant. "Sergeant," the colonel said, "please get the report filed by Corporal Montoya at the end of this expedition."

The sergeant got up and went into the outer office. While he was gone, the three men sat silently. Once the colonel said absently, *"Va a ser otro caliente hoy."* The two priests grunted noncommittally.

When the sergeant came back into the office, he was reading the corporal's report. He handed it to the colonel who himself read it carefully, sat it on his desk, and leaned back to look at the two priests. "Interesting report," he commented. "Have you read it?" Father Ibarra replied that he had, while Father de Landaeta said no. The colonel slid the report over to the superior.

While he was reading it, the colonel said, "I, of course, have read that report before. It never struck me that the corporal never actually says that Francisco died of disease. He says," here he picked up the report again, "early this morning the neophyte Francisco died suddenly. We buried him at the site, to avoid any spread of disease." He put the report down. "Where did we get the idea that it was disease that killed Francisco?"

Both priests looked at each other and said simultaneously, "Danti."

Finally Father de Landaeta spoke up. "That was always Father Danti's recitation of events. Father Danti told everyone that Francisco had gotten sick and died."

"Sergeant," the colonel said, "We need Corporal Montoya here immediately."

"Sir," the sergeant answered, and spun from the office.

Again, the other three sat silently. Finally, the colonel spoke to the superior. "We will have a detailed conversation with Corporal Montoya, Father. I think you need to plan such a conversation with Father Danti." Father de Landaeta nodded. Father Ibarra decided to interject.

"We are planning to bury Francisco's remains this afternoon, Colonel. Would you like us to delay this until you have had an opportunity to examine the evidence I have?"

"Let's see what the corporal has to say," the colonel answered.

As if on cue, Sergeant Amador stepped back into the office. "Corporal Montoya, sir," he said, gesturing to the figure behind him.

The corporal stepped into the office, looked at the group assembled and, without even being invited, slumped dejectedly into a chair.

"Corporal," the colonel began, "we have been reviewing your report of the patrol last March, in light of some evidence recently recovered." Once more he picked up the report. "Your report," he continued "says," and here he read carefully from the paper, "'Early this morning the neophyte Francisco died suddenly. We buried him at the site, to avoid any spread of disease.'" The corporal nodded grimly. The colonel continued levelly, "I must tell you, Corporal, that we have irrefutable evidence that the neophyte Francisco died of a gunshot wound. I wonder if you could tell me why your report does not reflect that not insignificant detail."

The corporal's head was almost on his chest, and he slowly shook it back and forth. Finally, he said, "It was an accident. No one meant to shoot him. Father Danti said that since only he and I knew how Francisco had died, we should keep it secret. There would only be trouble if it came out that he had been shot. 'Dead is dead,' he said. 'What does it matter how he has died?' No one had meant it to happen. Death by our own forces would only involve an investigation and questions on why we had been on the expedition in the first place. He told me not to put that he had been shot in my report and...I did not. I am sorry, sir." He raised his head and looked at the colonel. "I knew it was wrong at the time, and there is nothing I can do now but say I am sorry."

He was interrupted by the sergeant. "Corporal," he said, not unkindly, "I advise you to say no more at this time. You have some rights, and some interests to protect, and I advise you to say nothing until you have an *advocato* appointed to you."

The colonel fixed the corporal with a perplexed stare, and addressed his seargeant. "Sergeant," he said, "I want a court of inquiry convened in this office at eight o'clock tomorrow morning. I want Corporal Montoya and all his squad to be present at it. Father de Landaeta, I would like you and Father Ibarra to be here as well. Corporal Montoya, you are to consider yourself as under arrest and confined to the *presidio* grounds until further notice." He turned to the two priests. "You may conduct your burial service this afternoon. Please, what time will it be? I would like to be present."

"Thr...three o'clock?" Father Ibarra stammered.

"Three o'clock then. Until this afternoon, gentlemen." The colonel stood. Corporal Montoya and Sergeant Amador filed out together. The two priests thanked the colonel and left. The colonel sat and once more picked up the report to read again, slowly shaking his head.

As they began the walk back to the mission, Father Juan said to the superior, "I need to clear my head for a while. I think, while I am down this way, I will drop in on Xavier and see how his business and his new life is going. Please tell Estella of our plans for the burial and that I will be back before then." He turned and headed towards the town.

Xavier was jubilant at seeing the priest. "Come in, come in." He gestured grandly to a jumbled and dusty office. He offered the priest a seat and the inevitable cup of chocolate.

"How is the business going?" Father Juan asked.

"It is going wonderfully, Father. I am thinking seriously of hiring an assistant. I have more work than I can handle. There is a bank going in down by the waterfront, and they have given me the contract." He paused and smiled. "I am in the wonderful position of trying to decide whether I should hire an assistant first, or should I buy a cart and team first to move my material from job to job? I enjoy my life in town. I live above my shop," he gestured to the ceiling, "and no one tells me when to get up or when to go to bed or when to go to prayers." Here he shrugged and smiled apologetically. "To tell you the truth, I get to bed much later, and get up much earlier, than I ever did as a neophyte. When you work for yourself you are working for a slave driver!" He laughed. "But it is good, it is very good to be your own master." He gave the priest across from him a steady look. "But what about you, Father? I heard you have helped Estella to find her husband. She must be very happy."

Father Juan decided that this was not the time to go into the complexities of the search for Francisco's grave. He simply said, "We did find Francisco's grave. In fact, we are having a burial for him this afternoon at the mission cemetery. I think it would mean a lot to Estella if you would be there."

"I will most certainly, Father. What time?"

The two visited for most of the early afternoon. Xavier was reluctant to let his guest go, and nothing would do but that he take the priest to lunch. They went down to the wharf, where the fishermen were unloading their catch. It was once again a blazing hot day, and they sought the shade of a large warehouse that had just been completed. Xavier stopped in front of a woman who had a grill set up. She was offering tortillas and fish. It was, the priest admitted, the best meal he had had in a long time. Better than the plain, mostly vegetarian fare they had at the mission, and better by far than anything he had eaten on his trip to the *Rio San Joaquin.*

Finally, Father Juan was able to take his leave. "I must get back to the mission, Xavier. There are a few things to do before the service for Francisco. See you then." He walked back to the mission.

The service that afternoon was a brief and simple one. They gathered in the church where the basket with Francisco's remains was placed at the foot of the altar, and a requiem Mass was offered. Many of the neophytes were there, as well as Indians from the village. Francisco had been a popular and favored neophyte. All of the priests and brothers from the mission staff were there, including Father Danti. But the guest who got the most attention from all of those in attendance was Colonel Alberni, resplendent in a full-dress uniform and sword.

After the Mass, Xavier was chosen to carry the basket and lead the solemn group out the side door to the dazzling brightness of the cemetery. After a few more brief prayers, the basket was lowered into the ground. Estella, draped in a black mantilla, threw a handful of dirt into the grave. Father Ibarra reminded all, "Remember, man, thou art but dust, and unto dust thou shall return," and the service was concluded.

As the mourners began to disperse the colonel approached Estella. "Señora, if I may?" he said, sweeping off his hat and bowing slightly. He led her off some distance from the others and spoke to her for several minutes. She could be seen to nod slightly a few times, and finally the colonel bowed again and left.

31

As they walked out of the mission compound and down towards the *presidio* the next morning, Father de Landaeta surprised Father Juan by telling him, "I had an interesting item on my desk this morning, Juan." At the other's inquisitive stare, he continued. "It was a letter from Father Danti, requesting that he be transferred back to the College of San Fernando as soon as possible. He cited 'an intolerable dislike for these duties as they are presently assigned.'"

Father Juan did not know quite how to respond to this information, and the other gave him no real opportunity to. "I will forward it to Monterey with the next messenger." Father de Landaeta scoffed lightly, "It can languish there with my request until a decision is made. I do find the timing of it interesting, but I have given up speculation on such things."

When they had arrived at the colonel's office, the sergeant pulled Father Ibarra aside. "I think you should know, Father, that Father Danti visited the corporal last night. They had a very heated discussion. I could not hear what was being said, but they were clearly in disagreement, and once I heard the corporal shout, "No, no more lies!"

Father Ibarra was still puzzling over this when the two priests were called to a meeting room down the hall. Seated on benches in the corridor outside the room were the corporal's squad. Father Juan recognized Privates Galindo and Lopez, and Corporal Montoya. Galindo smiled broadly at the priest and greeted him warmly. The others remained sullen and undemonstrative. Inside the room itself, Colonel Alberni sat at the head of a long table. Sergeant Amador was to his left, and a guard stood at rigid attention at the door. The two priests were invited to take seats at the far end of the table on the other side. After a few preliminary remarks, the colonel asked the guard to bring in Private Lopez.

If the young soldier had been unsure and timid when he was talking with Father Juan several weeks ago, he was virtually speechless in front of the colonel. His story, when all was said and done, was essentially, "I know nothing, I saw nothing." He was quickly dismissed by the colonel.

Private Galindo was next. Again, he gave a clear picture of what had happened, with frequent references to his drawings, which the colonel had in front of him. His picture, though, as clear as it was, was still a picture of confusion, gunfire, and smoke. Other than what he had detailed on his map, he couldn't be sure where any of his comrades were during the battle.

Each of the other members of the squad were called in turn. Their stories were much the same: They had been marching in a column. When the runaways were spotted, everyone began running forward, gunfire erupted, and Francisco, and particularly where he had fallen, was behind them. Finally, the colonel called for Corporal Montoya." When the corporal had been administered an oath by the sergeant, the colonel began a formal intonation.

"Corporal, you are being called to offer your testimony regarding an incident of March third, last year. You, on that date, were in charge of a squad that was accompanying Father Antonio Danti in search of some runaway neophytes. Is that correct?"

"Yes, sir."

"You have already been advised, Corporal, that this court has been called to investigate two aspects of that expedition; is that correct?"

"Yes, sir."

"The first item this body must address are certain factual matters concerning a hostile action that occurred on that date, since it seems as if the after-action report you filed was not entirely truthful."

"Yes, sir."

"The second and more serious item to be considered is the death of an allied civilian at the hands of unknown members of the Spanish army."

Here the corporal leaned forward and began speaking animatedly. Sergeant Amador leaned over him and put a restraining hand on his arm, but the corporal just brushed it aside. "I have filed an incomplete and inaccurate report, and I am prepared to take the punishment for that. I will not have myself, nor any of my soldiers, accused of a deed that they did not commit. My squad that day was inexperienced and ill-trained, and they did not perform well. They did not, however, kill anyone."

"Corporal," the colonel interrupted him. "We have uncontroverted evidence that the neophyte Francisco was killed by a round fired from one of our weapons. I understand and admire your desire to protect your men. In fact, you very well may not know, and we may very well never find out, which of the men fired the fatal shot. But we must make our best effort to find out."

The corporal responded without hesitation. "It was Father Danti who fired the fatal shot."

There was an audible gasp from Father de Landaeta, and an open-mouthed stare from the colonel. Father Ibarra was not sure he understood, and Sergeant Amador smiled slightly. Finally, the colonel regained his composure.

"Please explain that very serious accusation, Corporal."

The corporal settled in his chair and his face took on a determined aspect. "We were marching in a somewhat irregular column. Well, we were *not* marching," he corrected, "we were *slogging* through very difficult terrain.

Several *varas* ahead of us were the neophytes, then was most of the squad, then Father Danti, Francisco and me. The runaways were spotted. This was when everything went to he. . ." He glanced at the two priests paying rapt attention. "That is, everything fell apart. Everybody started shouting, Father Danti more than anybody. 'Catch, them, catch them! They are getting away,' he screamed, and he began running forward until he was almost up to the main body of the squad. Francisco ran forward, too. He passed Father Danti. The rest of the squad was now spread out over perhaps fifty *varas*. Private Lopez was the very last soldier in the line, and he was abreast of Father Danti. He was confused about what to do, and stood there doing nothing, while the rest of the squad, and Francisco, continued to run forward. Father Danti began striking private Lopez. 'You're letting them get away, *stupido Indio*! Catch them, don't let them get away!' The runaways began disappearing into the brush. Francisco slowed down as he saw them escaping into the woods. It was then that Father Danti grabbed Private Lopez's musket and fired at the runaways. He hit Francisco; I saw Francisco get hit.

"When a man gets hit with a round fired that closely, he flies right off the ground. Father Danti's shot hit Francisco in the back. Then everyone began firing. I don't know how many rounds they fired. It was completely undisciplined. It is a wonder that none of the other neophytes were hit. I finally caught up to Father Danti and Private Lopez. The father still had the private's musket, and the private was crying. Private Lopez is a very simple man, sir, and he had no idea what was happening. He knew that practically the worst sin a soldier can commit is to let someone take his weapon.

"I took the musket from Father Danti and shoved it into the private's hands. I told him to reload and to move forward. I got the firing stopped, and told all the soldiers to stay where they were. Father Danti was still shouting at the others not to let the runaways escape. I grabbed him roughly, told him to shut up, and started to lead him to where Francisco lay. Just then, one of the neophytes started back toward us. I told him to stay where he was and when he continued toward us, I grabbed Lopez's musket and fired a shot over the neophyte's head. That stopped him!" the corporal smiled sardonically. "Poor Private Lopez, twice in one day someone took his musket away from him.

"I took Father Danti to where Francisco lay. He, Francisco, was completely still. He was completely dead," he said quietly, almost to himself. "His front, and the ground under him, were soaked with blood, but he was not bleeding any more. I told Father Danti, 'You shot him. I saw you shoot him.' Father Danti began sobbing and crying, 'Don't let anyone know, don't tell. No one saw but you. We'll just bury him and say he died of disease.' And," the corporal added with some finality, "that is what we did."

The colonel asked some more questions about blood and bloodstains, and the corporal explained that they had scuffed into the dirt any blood on the ground and wrapped Francisco's body in a blanket before calling the others back to help bury him. All anyone else saw was a blanket-wrapped body. "There is no one but me who has falsified this story," the corporal said. "None of my soldiers could have seen any of this except possibly poor Private Lopez, and I don't think he knows what he saw. My soldiers are not guilty of anything. Only I am."

"Only you, and Father Danti," Father de Landaeta corrected. The room was in shocked silence for several minutes. Finally, the colonel cleared his throat.

"I will consider all that we have heard and render a decision tomorrow. Corporal, you are to consider yourself still under arrest." He turned to the two priests. "As I am sure you know, Fathers, I nor any civil authority has any jurisdiction over any member of the clergy. Father Danti's guilt or innocence in this matter, and his punishment, if any, must be determined by an ecclesiastical court. I leave that matter entirely in your hands." He rose and left the room.

The two shocked priests got up and also left the room. As they walked back to the mission, neither one of them had much to say. Father Juan could not help but comment, "The fog is back; it is cooler. It seems as if our brief heat wave is over."

32

The very next day, Father de Landaeta called Father Danti into his office.

"Antonio," he began, "I want you to know that I will send your request for a transfer to the College of San Fernando with the next messenger going south."

"Good," the other monk replied. "I hope they act on it with dispatch."

"I am certain they will, Father, because that is not the only item I will send to Monterey with the next messenger." At the inquiring look from Father Danti, the superior continued. "As a result of evidence that has come to light, I am sending my recommendation that you be tried by an appropriate ecclesiastical tribunal for the death by misadventure of the neophyte Francisco on the expedition last March."

"Preposterous!" the other priest exploded. "I will not stand still for such an outrage. I will not let myself be subject to the calumnies of a bunch of *Indios*."

"Of course, Antonio," Father de Landaeta replied quietly. "That is the whole purpose of the trial I am recommending. To give you the opportunity to clear your name. I think it only fair to advise you as you prepare your defense that the charge is based not on the stories of any of the natives but on conclusive physical evidence, and perhaps most importantly on the sworn testimony of a noncommissioned officer of the king's army."

Father Danti started to reply further, thought better of it, and stood up abruptly. "When do I leave for Monterey?"

Father de Landaeta thought for a minute and replied, "Ordinarily, Antonio, we would wait for an answer to my letter to Monterey. However, I think in this case for all concerned we might do things a little irregularly. If we can get the *presidio* to arrange an escort to Monterey, we can send you, the escort and my message all at the same time."

"You mean you are going to send me to Monterey under arrest?" was the outraged response.

"Antonio, Antonio; you should know that is not the case. Neither I nor the military at the *presidio* have any authority to place you under arrest. We would not send any of our priests on a three-day journey without a military escort. You must know that. I thought from your question and your manner you could not wait to get started. Was I wrong?"

"No," the still ruffled priest replied. "I will make arrangements with the *presidio* to have a soldier escort me to Monterey."

Father de Landaeta advised him, not unkindly, "I must tell you that your name is not in particularly high favor at the *presidio* right now. I will arrange for an escort for you. I will go there today to do that and, if you would prefer, I would think you could probably be started today. Would that be agreeable?"

"Fine. I will get my things together and be ready to leave this afternoon."

The angry priest had hardly left the office when the superior left as well, to make one more trip down the hill to the *presidio*. It was mid-morning when he arrived there; he greeted Sergeant Amador and together they went in to see the colonel. The colonel and the sergeant were engaged in an intense conversation.

"I don't suppose, Father, this is just a social call?" the wary colonel asked.

"No, unfortunately, it is not," Father de Landaeta answered.

The colonel shook his head slowly. "Will we never see the end of this matter? The sergeant and I have just finished sentencing Corporal Montoya for his part in this debacle."

At the priest's concerned look, he reassured him. "We gave him a very light sentence. When all is said and done, from the military's perspective all Corporal Montoya did was file an incomplete report. When confronted with that, he accepted complete responsibility. He received the forfeiture of one month's pay. Since the corporal is not married and lives on the post, that should not be too much of a hardship."

The sergeant smiled. "What I told Father Ibarra some time ago holds true. The corporal is a good soldier and will make a good sergeant. He has learned a valuable lesson here: Don't let the influence of others affect your decision-making. He had misgivings about leaving the details of that death out of his report, and he let Father Danti's influence override his best judgment."

"That is what I am here about," Father de Landaeta began. "I am sending a message to Monterey recommending that Father Danti be tried by an ecclesiastical court for the death of Francisco. I would like that message, and Father Danti, to be gone from Mission San Francisco as soon as possible— not only for the mission's sake, but quite honestly for his own, as well. Once the story of Francisco's death becomes common knowledge, and we all know it will, I actually fear for Father Danti's safety."

"Sergeant, what do you suggest? Who do we send to escort the good *padre* back to Monterey? We already know he exerts an undue influence on our troop. I do not want to expose any more of them to his wiles." He looked apologetically at Father de Landaeta, who simply nodded in acknowledgement of the problem.

"I will escort him, sir," the sergeant suggested. "I will not be susceptible to his charms. He came very close to destroying one of my best soldiers, who is also a good friend. I will be happy to serve as the *padre's* escort to Monterey. When do we leave?"

"This afternoon?" Father de Landaeta asked. "Father Danti will be ready, and if you will stop by my office before you leave, I will give you my messages to go to the father president."

Once all arrangements were finalized, and **Father de Landaeta** found himself trudging back up the hill toward the mission once again, *I am getting too old for this sort of thing,* he thought.

When he got back to the mission, he sent for Father Danti, and told him that arrangements had been made for him to leave for Monterey that afternoon. Father de Landaeta could not quite read the expression on the other priest's face when he was told that his escort would be Sergeant Amador. As Father Danti turned to leave, the superior halted him. *"Vaya con Dios, Antonio."* He made the sign of the cross over him.

Just before noon, he asked one of the neophytes to have Father Juan report to him. When the other priest appeared, he updated him on all that had taken place. He told him of the sentence that had been pronounced on Corporal Montoya, and that Father Danti would be leaving for Monterey that afternoon, accompanied by Sergeant Amador; and that the sergeant would carry his recommendation for an ecclesiastical trial for Father Danti.

Father Juan asked if the sergeant could carry his report to the governor and the father president as well, on his findings regarding disease at San Francisco, and his findings regarding the death of Francisco.

"I am sure that will be fine, Father," was the superior's reply. "I know he is carrying the colonel's report as well. It is out of our hands now, Juan; we have done all that we can do."

"And what will they do at Monterey?" Father Juan asked.

The older priest shrugged resignedly. *"Lo. Que sera, sera."*

33

October had come, and with it the much-vaunted "best time of the year in San Francisco." As much as he disliked giving credit for being right about anything to Father Danti, who had caused so much turmoil at Mission San Francisco, Father Ibarra had to admit that he had been right about one thing: October *was* the best time of the year in San Francisco. Day after day dawned bright and clear. All day long a brilliant sun diffused the crisp air. Fog was a thing of the past, and although the weather was growing cooler, there was never what he would characterize as a cold day. The bay sparkled with brisk breezes. Not only the hills surrounding the bay, but the mountains beyond the hills were cleanly etched against a brilliant blue sky. He had been told that one morning he would wake up and see a mantle of snow on those distant mountains, and he would know, then, that winter was on its way.

Mission San Francisco had settled into a somewhat more benign routine. Sergeant Amador had returned with two messages from his trip delivering Father Danti to Monterey. One was to Father de Landaeta and referred to his "earlier request for transfer." The letter advised Father de Landaeta that "due to certain recent events at Mission San Francisco, of which you are undoubtedly aware, it is deemed impractical to grant your request at this time. You are to consider yourself as committed to Mission San Francisco de Assisi for the foreseeable future. Should you wish, a year from now, to submit a new request for transfer, it will be considered at that time."

Father de Landaeta had accepted this decision with equanimity and, as he told Father Ibarra, he was not surprised.

The second letter was to Father Ibarra. It went into profuse appreciation for his services and his investigative skills surrounding the "recent unfortunate death of one of our neophytes." It then used the exact same phrase as was in Father de Landaeta's letter: "due to certain recent events at Mission San Francisco, of which you are undoubtedly aware;" and continued to tell him that, "because there is now a shortage of priests at Mission San Francisco de Assisi, you will remain attached to Mission San Francisco, under the supervision of Father Martin de Landaeta. We will advise you when you are to return to Monterey." And like Father de Landaeta, he was not surprised, and not entirely displeased.

He had in the months since, established a pleasant routine. In the morning, he and Estella saw such of the neophytes as had ailments. They had started a small infirmary, and those who had disabling fevers or illnesses came under the care of Estella or one on the other neophytes they had trained to apply cooling baths or administer some of the simple medicines they had acquired. Afternoons he spent studying medical journals, instructing Estella, or occasionally visiting with the local shamans to learn from them some of the curatives they used. He was not hesitant to try them out as they recommended. Some he found no more or less effective than his own medicines, some he found, to his surprise, much more effective. One of his afternoon trips had been to the Miwok village on the other side of the bay, where he found that the herbal infusion that Guadalupe prescribed for Father de Landaeta was very likely cinchona. The shaman told him that it came from "far away; not Mexico, more south *terra de los Incas.*"

He had found Estella to be not just a very capable student, but a very good friend. As he instructed her in the ways of European medicine, she did not hesitate to enlighten him in the ways of natives. It was not long before he realized that she was held in very high esteem by her own people. Her unrelenting search for the truth about her husband's death had established her already in the local folklore.

As to Francisco's death, it was probably largely due to Estella's influence that in the minds of the locals it had since been forgiven, if not forgotten. Initially, when the truth had gotten out, there was much suppressed outrage, and even a few ineffective calls for revenge. Certainly, there were calls for justice. In fact, Estella herself had been a very effective leader of those calls. One day, several weeks after Father Danti had left San Francisco, she and Father Ibarra had discussed the issue.

"Father," she began, "it has been several weeks since Father Danti left for Monterey. When will his trial be, what will his punishment be?"

Father Ibarra had been dreading this conversation, but he had always known it was inevitable. "To tell you the truth, Estella, I don't know when it will be, or where it will be or even," here he paused and looking at her frankly, "if it will be."

"What do you mean, 'if' it will be?"

"As I think I explained to you, the civilian officials have no authority to try any priest. If a priest is accused of any misdeed or crime, he must be turned over to the church, and the church will conduct its own trial. Once the church does that, it may impose its own punishment. Again, it is under no obligation to report that punishment to anybody. If the church says, 'We have tried Father Danti and punished him,' that is the end of the matter. I don't know if Father Danti will be tried in Monterey or in Mexico, and I don't expect we will ever have a report back on that."

Estella answered with a resigned exhalation. "You know, Father, the church sometimes makes it very hard to be a Catholic. If I am caught in a sexual relationship with a man not my husband, even though neither I nor the man are married to anyone else, I will have my head shorn and be placed in the stocks, and the man will likely be flogged. If a priest, though, kills a man, nothing will be done."

"Be clear, my dear, I didn't say nothing will be done. I just said, we may never *hear* of anything that will be done."

Estella looked at him with what could only be described as pitying amazement. "I know what you said, Father; now listen to what I am saying: *nothing will be done.*" She had then immediately excused herself for the day, but the very next day a somewhat contrite Estella broached the subject again.

"I am sorry, Father, for my anger yesterday. I will tell you that I believe what I said and that nothing will be done. I was very angry about that, and I remained angry about it for a long time. I am still angry about it. On my way home, though, I stopped in the church. I prayed for an end to my anger, and I prayed for understanding. I am not sure *those* prayers were answered, but as you have taught us, prayers are *always* answered. I looked up at the crucifix and the twisted suffering Christ, and I remembered his words from the cross: 'Father, forgive them, for they know not what they do.'

"I think there has never been any idea that Father Danti knew what he was doing when he fired that musket. But I will be honest with you, Father; I have not forgiven him yet. He took my husband away from me. I have, though, accepted that I must keep trying to forgive him; and if I truly forgive him, what do I care what sort of punishment he receives?"

There was very little Father Juan could say to the amazing lesson in faith and humility he had just been given. He thought of Father de Landaeta's words so many weeks ago: "Perhaps we are not the only ones who have something to teach in this meeting of cultures." They had at that time been discussing physical ills, but it seemed as if the lesson applied equally to spiritual ones.

This was the last time Father Danti, or his punishment, or his future, ever came up between Estella and Father Juan. Information came to Father Juan many months later that Father Danti had been transferred to the College of San Fernando and made the novice master. He decided not to share this information with Estella, but when he mentioned it to Father de Landaeta, the other priest simply shook his head and muttered some comment about him "joining a long line of misfits prowling the halls of academe."

The gorgeous autumn had now given way to a wet and windy winter. Low-lying clouds of grayness obscured not just the hills around the bay, but oftentimes the bay itself. He had never seen the mountains in the distance coated with snow, but there was no doubt in Father Juan's mind that winter had come. The routine of the clinic, his studies, and the infirmary was a comfortable and not demanding one. He realized one day that he was more of a consultant to the clinic than an actual caregiver. Estella and her cadre of nurses had taken over virtually all the duties of the daily care of the sick. The sickness unfortunately continued, but one problem that was greatly diminished was that of runaways. There were still neophytes who decided that mission life was not what they had hoped it was, and who left to return to their own ways. There were, though, not nearly as many as there had been and when they disappeared, they were left alone to go, and welcomed back if they chose to return.

It was early November when the ship *San Jose* appeared in the harbor. The next day, a young Franciscan showed up in Father de Landaeta's office.

"Buenas dias, Padre," he greeted the superior, and knelt for a blessing. After receiving the benediction of the superior, he rose.

"I am Father Bartolome Virenza, Father. I am reporting to you to begin my service at Mission San Francisco de Assisi. Here is my letter of introduction from the father president." He handed the superior a sealed letter.

"Please have a seat, Father." The superior gestured towards a chair and sat down himself to read the letter. It was the usual letter of recommendation given when a young man started his career in the New World. It told of his background and education. It listed skills he had, and recommended him to "the care and supervision" of the addressee. The letter went on to mention that the *San Jose*, which had brought Father Virenza to San Francisco, would be undergoing repairs at San Francisco before returning to Monterey. It was expected that the repairs would take about two weeks. It then requested of Father de Landaeta that he "ensure that the Reverend Juan Jose Ibarra be prepared to return to Monterey with the *San Jose*, from whence he will proceed to Mission San Miguel to resume his regular duties."

Father de Landaeta put down the letter and realized that in a very short time he would be losing not just his priest/physician, but a very good friend.

"Welcome to Mission Dolores," he said to Father Bartolome.

¤ 34

It was Sunday morning and Father Juan was celebrating what he knew would be his last Mass at Mission San Francisco. There was no more denying what he had tried to ignore for the past two weeks: He would be leaving. He would leave with the *San Jose* and the flood tide on Tuesday, which he had been told would be about nine o'clock in the morning. As he was removing his vestments in the sacristy he glanced at the calendar. November 18. He hadn't even been in San Francisco for a year!

But so much had happened, it seemed much longer. He thought, as well, that he had only been in Alta California for three years. Three years and three missions! That could not be anyone's idea of stability. *I should have become a Benedictine*, he mused wryly.

He had one last "official" duty to attend to at San Francisco: A farewell party. When word had gotten out that Father Juan was being ordered back to *San Miguel*, nothing would do but he must be seen off with a grand fiesta. Whose idea it was originally, no one seemed to know, but the idea had been enthusiastically embraced by all, priests, soldiers, neophytes, gentiles, and town people. All wanted to be part of a farewell fiesta for Father Juan.

He headed over to the dining hall. The colonnade in front of it was decorated with brightly-colored pennants and flags, in the center of which was a large banner: *MIL GRACIAS A PADRE JUAN*. He stepped into a cacophony of voices and music. Estella was waiting just inside the door. Beaming, she grabbed his arm.

"Ah Father, I have been waiting for you. Now the party can begin." She stopped at a table to fill a cup of punch for him and then bustled him across the hall. Xavier was talking with an earnest young man who looked vaguely familiar. Xavier greeted him with an enthusiastic shout and a warm *abrazar*.

"Father, how good to see you! How sad to be seeing you only to say goodbye. But it is good for you, no? You will be going to *San Miguel* where you can resume the work you were sent here for, bringing relief to some of the suffering natives. Your talents will be better used." He turned to the young man beside him. "You remember Carlos Lopez, Father?"

Father Juan looked at the young man. He was stylishly dressed in an immaculate white tunic and tan calfskin trousers. His feet were encased in polished but plain working man's boots. His longish hair was held back from his face with a thin band, the same material as his trousers. He extended his hand and smiled at the priest.

"Uhm, I am sorry, I don't remember when we've met," the priest stammered.

Xavier's smile spread even wider across his face. "Carlos Lopez!" he said. "Private Lopez!"

Father Juan could not keep the gasping surprise from his face.

"You, you..."

"I know, Father, I do not look the same." He added happily, "I am not the same. The army decided to rid itself of me after the unfortunate affair with Father Danti. 'You will never make a soldier, Lopez,' the sergeant told me. 'You are a good man, but you will never make a soldier. We are discharging you with honor and one month's pay and we hope you will be able to find your calling.' That was the best thing that ever happened to me, Father. I found a job as Xavier's assistant and we discovered I have a talent for sculpting and stone carving."

"And what a talent!" Xavier interrupted. "Now I am not just a stone mason; I am able to offer fine carving for doors and lintels, and statutes for gardens, and" here he paused and gave a wink, "tombstones! Everyone will eventually need a tombstone, and everyone in San Francisco wants one of Carlos' tombstones. Carlos is not just my assistant. He will soon be my partner!" He held up his hand as if framing a sign on the wall. "Ibarra and Lopez: Purveyors of Fine Stone Monuments and Decorative Items." As he threw his arms around both Father Juan and the beaming young man, Estella stepped forward. She put a hand on Xavier's arm.

"*Carita,* Father Juan must visit with some other people."

Carita? Father Juan thought, as she took him over to two people he did recognize: Oralia and Private Galindo. Here there was no second-guessing as to terms of endearment. The private had his arm possessively and firmly around Oralia's waist.

"*Padre!*" Oralia greeted him, and placed an impulsive kiss on his cheek.

"How good to see you, my dear, and you, too, Miguel...or should I go back to calling you 'private?'" he asked with a smile.

Oralia pulled back from the soldier a bit and turned his arm toward the priest. "You should be calling him 'corporal!'" she squealed, pointing to the two chevrons on his sleeve.

"Ah, congratulations, congratulations, Corporal. Certainly, a well-earned promotion."

Castano was next in the introductions Estella took him through. The old man was beaming and visiting with Father Virenza and telling him of his work with Father Palou. The young priest was clearly impressed to meet someone who had known a companion of Junipero Serra. In fact, he glanced at Father Juan with a look that clearly asked, *Is this true?*

"It's true," Father Juan said. "Castano knew the Reverend Father Palou when he was at San Francisco twenty years ago. Did you know, Father, that it was here in San Francisco that Father Palou wrote the first book ever written in California?" Feeling the frivolity and conviviality of the afternoon, and perhaps the cup of strong punch he added, "Castano helped him write it." The old man smiled and nodded.

As Estella now guided him toward the sergeant and the colonel who were standing off together, it suddenly struck Father Juan: Everyone who had been on that expedition to the swamps with him was there except one.

He turned to Estella. "Estella, where is your baby? Where is young Francisco?"

"Oh, Father," she reassured him. "He is fine, he is growing now so he doesn't need to be with me at all times. He is in Father de Landaeta's office. Father de Landaeta has let us set a little basket up for him there, and I have a young girl who will sit with him and watch him and call me if he needs anything."

The afternoon and the party continued in a whirl of meetings, introductions, and reminisces. Father de Landaeta reminded him of how suspicious he had been of him when he first arrived.

"And now, Juan," he said tremulously, "I am truly sorry to see you go."

Corporal Montoya actually thanked him for "forcing me to do what I knew was the right thing. I don't think I could have lived with myself for the rest of my life knowing that I had hidden the truth about how that boy died."

Finally, the afternoon and the evening wore down. The guests began leaving. Father Juan would be glad to see the last one go, because he was getting tired. Estella came up to him. She once more had her infant in his sling. Xavier stood by the door, clearly waiting to escort her from the party.

"I don't know if I will see you before you leave for Monterey, Father. I want to thank you for all you have done for me and for Francisco." It was not clear if she was referring to her husband or her baby. It was not important. "I want to thank you for all you have done for poor Mission Dolores. I want to thank you for all you have done for my people. Please, Father, your blessing for me and my child." She bowed her head and pulled the blanket back from the sleeping child's face. Father Juan intoned a soft prayer and made the sign of the cross over mother and child. Her eyes were glistening as she turned toward the waiting Xavier.

Father Juan could not resist. He put a slightly restraining hand on Estella's arm and nodded his head towards Xavier. *"Carita?"* he asked.

Estella smiled through tear-filled eyes. "Carlos is preparing a tombstone for Francisco. When it is finished and in place, Xavier and I will be married. *Vaya con Dios, Padre."*

1. Mission San Francisco de Assisi is now located in the heart of downtown San Francisco. In 1795 though, the mission, now the oldest building in San Francisco, and the Presidio below it were the only two distinguishing features of the "city by the bay." Get a picture of San Francisco from the Bay, today. Imagine it with none of those buildings there.

2. Almost as soon as he arrives at Mission San Francisco Father Juan Ibarra is made aware of the fact that while he is a Franciscan priest, just as are the caretakers of the Mission, he is going to find himself in conflict with those other priests. Why is that?

3. What is it that makes Father Juan different from all of the other Franciscan priests in California?

4. Estella, a young mother comes to Father Juan with a problem she expects him to resolve. Are her expectations the naïve hopes of an unsophisticated young woman? Are his doubts the cynical response of a callous member of the ruling class?

5. Father Juan gets two very different stories of a previous disastrous expedition to the inland waterways of San Francisco Bay. Which is he initially inclined to accept?

6. Eventually he comes to believe that the "official" story is not correct. What is it or who is it that changes his view of the events?

7. Throughout the book there is a decided "disconnect" between the Franciscan's view, and the natives' view of how the mission is being run. What is your first take on these two views? What is your final take? Which was likely the correct view?

8. Sickness and disease play a major role in the events of this book. Does it make sense that things such as a common cold, flu, measles could have had such an impact on this settlement?

9. Estella is an obedient, perhaps even docile member of Mission San Francisco. She ultimately decides to take matters in her own hands. This precipitates a major crisis at the mission and a major turning point in the book. Is it realistic to expect this young woman to embark on the course of action she does? What about Father Juan's observation that perhaps she had learned her religious lessons too well?

10. Father Juan as he embarks on the search for Estella, finds himself recruiting as an ally another young woman, Oralia. There are major differences though between Estella and Oralia. What are some of those?

11. Through much of this story the Spanish army is cast as an evil oppressor. But it is a member of the Spanish army who ultimately finds Estella and reunites her with her friends. Who is this? What are the circumstances which lead to his transformation?

12. On the expedition to the inland, Castano is a bit of an anomaly. He is an old man. He is not one who will seriously contest the Spanish army. He is not a mission neophyte. He seems to bring little to the problem of finding Estella. What role does Castano play in the search and in the story?

13. Estella finally gets an answer to her question, "what happened to Francisco?" It is an unexpected and transformative answer. What does she do with the information? Is justice done?

14. This book is set very late in the 18th Century in the greater San Francisco Bay Area. In the 300 years since the events of this book very much has changed in that area, and yet very much has remained the same. The Bay, its outer reaches, the tides, the two great rivers feeding into it operate pretty much the way they always have. Look at a map of the San Joaquin Delta. Imagine yourself as a 20-year-old woman, trying to find her way through that area. without signs, commercial establishments, houses, piers or wharves. There are only water, reeds, and low lying islands.